T0210117

THE MAN
OF GOD

A Story about Forgiveness

A NOVEL BY
W. R. COLEMAN

authorHOUSE®

AuthorHouse™
1663 Liberty Drive
Bloomington, IN 47403
www.authorhouse.com
Phone: 1 (800) 839-8640

Published by AuthorHouse 01/23/2020

ISBN: 978-1-7283-4451-5 (sc)
ISBN: 978-1-7283-4452-2 (e)

Library of Congress Control Number: 2020901293

Print information available on the last page.

This is Dedicated to My Family:

My Ancestors – their Prayers protect me.

My Elders – their Steadfastness supports me.

My Father – his Wisdom teaches me.

My Mother – her Strength amazes me.

My Sisters – their Beauties dazzle me.

My Nieces & Nephews – their Laughter blesses me.

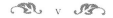

CHAPTER 1

IT WAS ALWAYS KIND OF like stepping back in time, going home. Not because the places had not changed, because they had. The stores were bigger and the streets were wider. The new high school was built only a few years earlier and combined all the county schools at one site. A major chain store was built on front street and became the mecca for weekend socializing. The inertia manifested itself not in the streets of the city, but in the hallways and bedrooms and kitchens and dens of every house he visited. And especially in his relatives' houses. He was eternally "ManMan." They all knew his real name – Rayford Telifero Johnson, Jr. – he was named after his father. But not since he was baby had anyone in his family called him anything but ManMan. He had always been the good son. The one who would go to college, finish, and make the family proud.

There was one other thing of which everyone

was sure: there was no question in anyone's mind, except maybe his, that he would be a preacher. From as early as he could remember, people had been telling him, "You gonna preach the Word one day, Son. I can see it all over you." Or, as somebody had said to his mother one Easter Sunday, "Sister, you take good care of this boy. I hear the voice of a preacher there." He wasn't particularly concerned about it when he was young. He just knew that he liked the attention and praise after one of his "fiery" prayers or when he acted like Rev. Gardner at the family Christmas dinner. The "Calling" was something that he didn't even understand as a child. But when he was fifteen, he too began to realize that there was something special on him and in him.

It was during Vacation Bible School at the church. ManMan had been asked to help out during the week. All the younger children looked up to him, and he didn't mind. It would get him out of the house, and he would get to see Marie, his "girl friend," everyday. One of the seven-year-olds named Travis had been causing trouble all week and by Friday, everybody knew that even Mrs. Jenkins was tired of him. She was the most patient person in the church and always volunteered to plan VBS activities. If a parent was late picking a child up, Mrs. Jenkins would wait or take the child home herself. She never fussed. She would always bring the children to order with one question: "Now if Jesus walked through that door, would He be happy to see you acting like this?" In a few seconds, even the rowdiest children would be in their seats. But this Travis was the exception.

On Friday, the last day of VBS, there was a barbeque at the lake. The children ran and played until it was time to eat. Everyone was finally served and eating when one of the children asked, "Where is Travis?" Mrs. Jenkins stopped pouring punch and began to a headcount. "42, 43, 44." There should have been forty-five children. After they had looked in the restrooms and anywhere else Travis could have been hiding, ManMan and the other three teenagers were sent by twos in different directions to search. One of the other adults stayed with Mrs. Jenkins who tried to act calm, but she was obviously very concerned. They all hoped this was just another one of Travis' pranks and that he would pop from around some corner, grinning, saying, "I fooled ya'll again."

ManMan and Marie went toward the lake. They tried to talk everything into being okay. "You know he's somewhere looking at us, saying how stupid we are," Marie began.

ManMan replied, "I know, and when we find him, I think I'll ask Mrs. Jenkins if I can call his

Mama. You know she said if we had anymore trouble with him, just let her know." Travis' mother was a member of the church, but no one had ever seen his father.

"I don't think she can handle this boy. He's so bad!" Marie was about to continue when they reached the lake and saw it at the same time. There was something red in the water. Travis had been wearing a red shirt and some blue jeans. Marie looked at ManMan, who had already pulled off his shoes and shirt. Before she could say anything, he was running toward the water. "Go tell Mrs. Jenkins to call 911." With that, he was in the water.

As he swam toward the red place in the water, ManMan prayed. He didn't even really think about it. The words just came. "*By Your Spirit, God. Hold his life in Your hand, God. He shall live and not die. By Your Spirit, God. He shall live and not die. He shall live and not die.*" Then he was there. The red spot was Travis. His body was limp and cold. By what surely was God's plan and purpose, ManMan had spent the early part of the summer taking life-guard classes. He thought it was so he could work at the Y and make a little money during the summer. But now, as he swam back to the bank of the lake with Travis' lifeless body in tow, ManMan realized God knew the real purpose for the classes. And it had nothing to do with making money.

When he reached the bank, his training kicked in. He listened for breath while looking for chest movement. None. Next step – CPR. Breath, chest compressions. Wait. Breath, chest compressions. Wait. Give Travis' body time to work. Nothing. Breath, chest compressions. Breath, chest compressions. Wait. Nothing. Pray. *"Holy Spirit, breath through me. Breath through me, God. He shall live and not die. In Jesus' Name, breath through me."* Breath, chest compressions. Breath, chest compressions. Wait. Breath. Breath. Breath. Deep breath – Travis' breath. Travis' little body began to shiver as his lungs forced him to cough and expel the water that had filled them. As Mrs. Jenkins and the paramedics ran toward the lake, ManMan tried to calm the child. "It's okay, man. Just be still. You all right. You just fine."

When they asked him what had happened, Travis said he couldn't remember. He was just standing on the edge of the water, and then he wanted to swim. So he did. Never mind the fact that he *couldn't*. But he did remember when he heard somebody praying, "just like Uncle Columbus do on Sunday before we have to go to children's church." Mrs. Jenkins asked what the person said when they were praying. Travis said, "He shall live and not die. He shall live and not die. He shall live and not die.

That's what he said, Mrs. Jenkins. That's what he said."

At that point, ManMan began to consider the true Power of God and this Calling thing. He had told everyone about swimming out to Travis, bringing him back to the bank, using his lifeguard training to do CPR, even about how Travis began to breathe again and cough to get the water out of his lungs. But not one time had he mentioned praying while he was swimming or when he was performing CPR. He knew God had heard him, had answered his prayer, had honored His Word, but he hadn't told anybody. Not even Marie or Mrs. Jenkins. And surely not Travis. So how had he heard the words? He was unconscious. He wasn't even breathing when ManMan got him out of the water. How had he heard the prayer?

The questions stayed on ManMan's mind and Sunday, as Rev. McNeil preached, something else he could not explain happened. He was sitting in his regular seat, not in the choir stand because the Senior Choir was singing that day. He was just sitting there, listening to Rev. McNeil, wanting more and more to shout or run or something. His face began to burn. He was sure Marie could see it. She was sitting right beside him, so he turned his face toward the wall. That didn't help, though. Something was happening – and ManMan knew what it was: the Spirit of God was on him. He wanted to go outside or to the restroom or somewhere. He wanted to, but he couldn't.

"You wondering what it is. You wondering how the impossible happened. You wondering how a child could drown, die, no life in his body – how he could be brought back to his mama's arms alive and well. 'Not by power, nor by might, but by My Spirit, saith the Lord.'" Rev. McNeil was saying exactly what ManMan had been thinking since Friday. The tears were rolling down his cheeks faster than he could wipe them, and he was sure Marie saw him crying. So he didn't try to hide anymore. To his surprise and relief, she was crying, too. They both looked across the church, near the front, and saw Travis' mother rocking back and forth. She would shout soon. And ManMan felt like he would, too.

He grabbed Marie's hand and squeezed it, hoping that she would anchor him. Keep him from shouting or running or whatever was going to happen next. But it didn't help. ManMan was on his feet before he knew it. He just had to stand and be a witness to the Power of God that moved through him to save Travis' life and that flowed over him at that very moment. So he stood there, not worrying about everybody seeing the tears or seeing his hands raised in honor and in surrender.

He stood there and was not ashamed. That was the day, almost twenty years ago, that he knew whatever God wanted or needed him to do or be – Rayford Telifero Johnson, Jr. accepted the Call to be a Man of God.

CHAPTER 2

THAT WAS ALSO THE SUMMER Marie was sure she had fallen in love. Unfortunately, it was not with ManMan. She thought just because Jerome had come from the city, just because he was going to be a senior when school started, just because he was something new – he was something better. So she spent less and less time with the boy she had known all her life, and by the time school started, everybody knew she was "Jerome's girl." As for ManMan, he tried not to let it bother him. He figured Marie would get tired of Jerome, maybe. Or he would get tired of her. Then she would start calling again. And he would forgive her and take her back.

When he began to hear the rumors going around the school after Christmas break, he took up for Marie and said the rumors were just that: rumors. He knew she wouldn't, couldn't let herself be fooled by that fast-talking, shifty-eyed, slick-haired Negro

from Chicago. She had always told him, "I want me a husband from right here in Waynesboro. So when we get married, he won't be saying 'you from the county, so you must *be* country.' If we both from here, we'll both be country together." That's what she had always said. ManMan just knew Marie couldn't be quitting school. She couldn't be marrying this city boy. She couldn't be leaving Mississippi before it was time for them to go to college. Most of all, she couldn't be pregnant with his baby.

Then about two weeks after their 16th birthday (he and Marie were born on the same day, the same year), ManMan's mother was on the phone talking to Mrs. Carter, Marie's mother.

"Well, Honey, you can't ever tell what will happen. But don't you sit there and blame yourself. You raised that child well, and then, without a husband, too. You did good, Baby. And she go' be alright. Whether she marry that boy or not, she go' be alright 'cause we all go' be right here to help both of you. Don't you hold your head down, and don't let her hold hers down, either." His mother's words were consoling but her face was wet with tears. She was like a second mother to Marie, as was Mrs. Carter to him. Both mothers were hurt, but neither could let the other, or the children whom they were discussing, hear or see their hurt. When she saw ManMan standing in the kitchen door, Mrs. Johnson tried to change the subject. But he had already heard the part of the conversation that gave validity to the rumors. They were no longer such, but were now the truth.

All of these memories flooded his mind as he cruised down the interstate. After about the fourth hour, he was tired – of the memories and of driving – and began to rethink his decision to drive instead of fly. He could have been home by now. By driving, he reasoned, he could always leave right after the funeral, using the excuse that "it's a long drive and I've got to be there on Monday." And, if things still didn't feel right after he saw his daddy, he might stay a few extra days. Something in his father's voice had almost trembled, almost faltered as he asked ManMan to come to the funeral. The son could hear something distinct and almost desperate in that one question, "You coming home for the funeral?" He did not know what was going on, but the uneasiness in the bottom of his stomach told him to be ready for it.

The next exit, with food, gas, restrooms, was only about twenty miles further. He could hold on until then, although the urge to pull over and get a good nap did appeal to him. The scan button on the radio was his best friend during these long trips. The cassettes and CDs were too familiar and didn't offer sufficient variety to keep his mind occupied. The radio did, at least, keep him guessing and amused with "the hottest mixes" and stupid commercials. Country station. Country station. Jazz station — remember that number. Hip-hop. Rap. Classical. Country station. Anita ". . . *it's been you all the time*."

That's good right there. That song took him back to the first time he heard it. The tape had come in the mail to him in an envelope. No return address. The postmark was from home, so he figured Jeannine, his sister, had sent him her latest demo. Her voice was like satin around your body and chocolate going down your throat. She had done at least three demo tapes, but couldn't make up her mind whether she wanted the almost guaranteed success and fortune of an R&B career, or the perhaps less glamorous, "right thing to do with her gift" gospel career. So when he opened the padded envelope and saw the words "From My Heart to Yours" typed on the label, he still thought it was from Jeannine. The title was ambiguous enough to go either way. ManMan was in no particular hurry to listen to the tape, but he figured he better because the second phase of the process would be a phone call from Jeannine and a lengthy conversation about the quality and marketability of her latest work.

The voice he heard on the tape was not his little sister's. It was instead a tried-by-the-fire, lived-to-tell-about-it, came-out-as-pure-gold, wrestled-with-the-angel-for-her-voice-and won Anita Baker. The refrain *"it's been you all the time"* told him the tape could only be from one person, at home or elsewhere: Marie, or May as they called her. It had been only a year and a half since he left home then, more than three since she had left with Jerome. But by no stretch of the imagination were they still in any kind of relationship. Jerome didn't like her talking to ManMan, and Marie abided by his wishes. Besides, it was long distance to call him from Chicago. At the end of the triple-play version of the song, he heard Marie's voice. It was sad and almost empty, but it was her voice. With very little emotion and no hint of sensuality, the voice said: "You know it's you. I know it's you. Why are we pretending we don't?" That's all. He looked at the postmark again. Yes, it was from Mississippi. But why was Marie sending something from Mississippi? He didn't know but knew who would.

He called home, hoping that Jeannine would answer the phone instead of his mother. Not that he didn't want to talk to his mother, but Jeannine would have the information he needed and would tell him *everything.* What she did tell him was more than he was ready to hear. As it turned out, Marie had come back home about a year earlier. She had missed his departure for college by only about three weeks. Everybody was shocked to see her, to say the least. She had been calling her mother faithfully every month or so, saying how wonderful everything was and how happy she, Jerome, and the baby were. They were all healthy and happy as could be. The baby was growing like a weed, and Jerome was about to get a promotion at work. All was well.

When she showed up in Mississippi without Jerome – or the baby – it couldn't have been a sign of anything good. It was about three o'clock in the morning when her mother heard something on the porch. She figured it was the cat running from the dog so she didn't pay much attention to it. She turned over and soon heard a knock so faint that it could have been a child's. Sitting up on the side of the bed, she listened hard. Yes, somebody was knocking on the door at, what was it? 3:00 in the morning? Her slippers were at the side of the bed and she hurriedly pulled on her old housecoat. It must be an emergency. Something must have happened. "*Lord, have mercy, Jesus,*" she automatically began to pray. "*Oh, bless, Lord, in the Name of Jesus. Bless Lord.*" There was no way she could have known how much more she would have to pray in the next few weeks to snatch her child from the very gates of hell.

"Who is it?" Mrs. Carter expected to hear the voice of one of the neighborhood children. She stopped and listened. "Who is it, I say?" No answer. She flipped the porch light on and went to the window. She couldn't see anybody, but the window only provided a partial view of the porch. If someone was standing close to the door, they couldn't be seen. She stood still and, after a few seconds, had almost convinced herself that no one had knocked at all. She had probably been dreaming. She flipped the switch to turn the light off and headed back down the hall to her room. Before she got to the corner, she heard the knock again, this time more determined than the first.

"Who is it, I say?" By this time, she was thinking about what was near her that she could use as a weapon. The heavy pillar candle on the piano. The beautiful vase she had gotten for Christmas. She would hate to break it, but would if she had to. Her walking cane. It wouldn't do much damage, but it would make the intruder think again by the time she got through hitting him upside the head with it.

"Mama, it's me." The voice was small and as faint as the first knock had been.

"It's me, Mama. Open the door."

Mrs. Carter couldn't believe her ears. She knew

that her only child, her Marie, should be in Chicago with her husband and baby. And yes, some of the other young women and girls in the neighborhood called her "Mama." But a mother always knows her child's voice. This was the child she had birthed, and this child was hurting.

It seemed like her hands wouldn't move fast enough to release the chain and undo the lock. She fumbled with them until finally she opened the door and was face to face with her beautiful child. It was obvious, though, to this mother, that something was wrong. The quiver she thought she heard in Marie's voice was confirmed by the sadness in her bloodshot eyes. They stood looking at each other for several seconds like they were seeing ghosts. It was Marie who broke the silence, but not with words. She fell into her mother's arms and let out a soul-wrenching cry that surely rivaled the one Mary made at the foot of the cross. This mother could not support her child. Her soul was heavy with pain. So they both sank to the floor. At first they were on their knees embracing. Then Marie sank a little lower, almost laying down right there at the front door. But this mother would not have it. She made it to the floor before her child did, and, cradling Marie in her arms, rocked and prayed for the next three hours. She didn't know what had weighed her child down so heavily, but she did know that God knew. So she talked to Him on behalf of her child: *Father, I don't know what it is. I don't know what happened. I don't even know when it happened, God. But I know You know. This is my child, Lord, and You got to help her. You know all and You see all. You are the God of all. You the only one can help her through whatever this turn out to be. Oh, God, by Your Holy Spirit, I want You to come right now and hold this child. I can't do it by myself, God. Wrap Your arms around her and me both, Father. Jesus, make intercession for her. If she done wrong, plead her case. If she been done wrong, move on her heart to heal it. Holy Ghost, this is my child. The only one I got, and I'm trusting You to bring some comfort. Do it, Lord, in the Name of Jesus . . .* She prayed that way for those three hours, holding Marie there on the floor by the front door.

CHAPTER 3

THERE WAS NO FANFARE WHEN ManMan made it home. It was well after midnight, and only his mother was awake. He knew she would be until he actually made it. She met him on the front porch and waited patiently as he got his bags out of the trunk. As he made it to the porch, a tremendous peace came over him. He always felt like that in his mama's presence. He looked forward to it. And it never failed to be.

"Hey, Baby, we been waiting for you. Well, I been waiting for you. Everybody else done gone to bed."

"Hey, Mama. Yeah I finally made it," he said, hugging her tightly and stopping to let her hold his face in her hands. She also did this every time he came home. She seemed to study his face, his eyes really, and read in that few seconds everything he didn't even have the words to tell. She kissed him on the cheek and led him into the house.

"How was the drive? You hungry? I got some meat and peas ready, and the cornbread just need to be put in the oven. By the time you put your stuff up and maybe wash up, it'll be ready."

He had not eaten on purpose – he knew just as surely as she would be waiting up, his mama would have a hot meal ready for him, too.

"The drive was okay. Just long. I got tired and had to stop and sleep for about 30 minutes. That's why I'm late and hungry. Go ahead and put the bread in the stove. I'll be ready when it gets ready." He loved his mother so much, and he understood that feeding him, no matter how old he got and how long he stayed away, was one of her favorite ways to express her love for him. So after he put his bags in "his room" and washed his face and hands, he sat down at the table opposite his beautiful mother.

I pray that my wife will be a lot like Mama, he thought to himself. She didn't have to be and likely would not be a homemaker. She would probably have a job she went to everyday. Some days she would cook dinner, but many times he would. She might come home from work before he did, but she would work overtime on many days, too. She would want children, but would plan together with him when they would start their family. In terms of her daily activities, his wife would probably not be like his mother, but in her spirit she must be nothing less than his mama's example. Kind. Honest. Generous. Strong. Understanding. Unconditionally loving. Yes, Mrs. Rayford T. Johnson, Jr. would have these same spiritual, emotional gifts with which his mother had showered him all his life.

"What did the folk at work say when you told them you were taking time off? I know they liked to cried." Her words jarred his mind back to the table.

"Yeah, everybody had a million questions. 'Well, what about this report?' 'What about the Friday conference?' 'What about going to the bathroom?'"

His mother was laughing out loud at Rayford's mimicry of his employees as she checked on the cornbread. It was almost ready. She stirred the peas, still laughing, and came back to the table.

"Say they go' be lost, Baby?" She could not, nor did she try to hide her pride. ManMan had finished college and grad school, and a month after graduation, had opened his own architecture company. She wasn't sure of what all that entailed, but she knew "her baby sho' could build some pretty big ol' houses! Just look at mine!" she would always say.

"They'll be alright. I just hope the company will!" He was joking, of course. He had been blessed with some of the best and brightest minds in the field. The company was doing quite well. Business was, as they say, booming. And he was very grateful not only to God, but to his mama and daddy for all their sacrifice. That's why the third house he designed and built was theirs. And it was third, not first or second, only because he had to have "some money to work with."

He had tried to remember all of the things his mama liked about the old house and all of the little or large nuances she admired about others' homes. Like the little room off to the side of the kitchen for her flowers. And the huge sunken den with a splendid cathedral ceiling. He had told her to start a list when he began grad school. By the end of the third year, on the day of his graduation, he asked her for it. Surely enough, she went to her Bible on the bedroom table and pulled out a somewhat frayed piece of notebook paper. She looked the list over one more time, added two wishes, and gave it to him. The only wish on the list that he did not personally fulfill was that for a "big, pretty flower garden with all kind of flowers in it." He made sure the landscapers left a space and enclosed it with a beautiful 12-inch high white picket fence border, but the actual planting he left to her. Rayford knew his mama, and she would NOT be happy with a manufactured flowerbed. She would rather do it herself. And she did.

"I had to get up and see if Mama was alright in here laughing by herself." Jeannine squinted to get a good look at ManMan. She had taken her eyes out before going to bed.

"My, God, the dead had arisen!" Rayford and Jeannine knew the reference to *The Color Purple*, and she responded by putting the finger on him. They hugged, and she joined him at the table.

"And what's wrong with laughing by yourself?"

"Mama, I didn't say nothing was wrong with it. Just don't be doing it out in public."

"Aw, hush, Smarty." Jeannine's disposition was much like her brother's. She had a sharp wit and an even sharper mouth. Mrs. Johnson knew it and couldn't be the least bit upset because she had the same problem as a girl growing up and as a young single woman and as a young married woman. So she was very familiar with a smart mouth to say the least.

"What took you so long to get here, Boy? Don't you know better than to come in here, talking all loud, waking everybody up?"

"As bad as you look, you should have stayed in the bed. You need all the beauty rest you can get. I do believe you done got uglier since the last time I was home." ManMan had not gotten the last word out of his mouth good before Jeannine splashed some water in his face, the little bit that remained in a glass sitting on the table.

"You know you will reap that more times than you can stand, don't you? When you least expect it."

The two of them had never really grown up to the point where they weren't constantly ragging on each other. But there were other times when their interactions and conversations were devoid of laughter and joking, and were so thick and deep until they could only talk in whispers — even when they walked down the road and there was no chance for anyone but God to hear them. Like the time she told him that Sammy Warford had tried to force himself upon her.

"What do you mean 'force himself on you'?" ManMan had tried to be calm until he understood fully what she meant. He didn't want to make her uncomfortable with his anger.

"Well, we went to the movies and then to his house. . . . And don't look at me like that, I know I shouldn't have been in his house. But I thought he was okay. Anyway, I told him I was ready to go. Well, after we kissed and stuff. And he said, 'Okay, go get the keys off the bed.' I went, and when I turned around, he was right behind me."

"And what did he do?"

"He said, 'Since we're back here, we might as

well do a little something before you go.' I said, 'Sammy, you crazy. You know I ain't fixin' to do nothing, with you and nobody else.' And I went to go around him, but that nigger pushed me on the bed and before I knew anything, he was on top of me."

"And what did he do then?" That was the only thing ManMan could say and still pretend that he was not furious and already planning what he would do to Sammy.

"I said, 'Sammy, if you don't let me up, you better. Have you lost your mind? Let me up, nigger!" He just looked me in my face and said, 'You know you want it. Why you come up in my house if you didn't want some of this? I'm go' give you what you want, Baby J.' And then I just started fighting and hollering. I scratched, slapped, kicked, punched, anything I could do. I tried to beat the hell out of him. He was stronger than me, though. He had me pinned down on the bed, and then I grabbed his chain. I snatched it from around his neck and he finally stopped. 'I know you ain't broke my chain! I know damn well you ain't broke my chain!' He felt around his neck and wiped some blood off where the chain had cut him and went to the bathroom to get a towel. I ran out the house, got in his car, and went home."

ManMan almost laughed at her ingenuity for

taking the car and praised her strength for fighting back, but his sister was still visibly shaken by what had almost happened. They both knew Sammy, had gone to school and church with him. But that did not make a difference to him, or to ManMan. He knew he would get up early the next morning and go find Sammy. Once found, he would beat him mercilessly and without a care in the world about how many times they had fought bullies together or how he and Sammy were practically brothers-in-law because he was Marie's brother.

And that is exactly what he did. That Sunday morning he packed his stuff in the car, kissed his mother, shook hands and hugged his father, and said to his sister, "Watch where you go and who you go with, but keep fighting, too. I'm going to get mine in this morning." It took Jeannine a few minutes to realize what he was saying, but when she saw Sammy a few days later, she understood clearly. Both of his eyes were swollen shut, he had his arm in a splint, he walked with a limp, and when he saw Jeannine coming, he immediately went the other way. He remembered the last thing ManMan had said to him before he blacked out, "The next time you see my sister, you better go the other way, nigger."

CHAPTER 4

"Wake up, ManMan. Wake up. It's somebody here to see you." His mother's voice in the morning always reminded Rayford of getting ready for school. He didn't give her much trouble, and she didn't have to call him twice unless it was the first or the last day of school. All of the days in-between were okay, but the first day of school always brought with it the uneasy feeling of almost-nausea and mutant butterflies flying around in his stomach. On the last day of school, he was so glad it was almost over for a while and he could finally go to work. He wanted to stay in bed all day just to celebrate. His mama's voice early in the morning always sent him back. Or at least he thought it was early in the morning. He turned over and looked at his mother, who was smiling, and then at the clock - 10:49.

He must have been more exhausted than he thought. Then again, he and Jeannine had stayed up until about 5:00 in the morning talking about this and that. She had mentioned she was in the process of getting back in school. As much as Rayford hated to admit it to himself, he knew not to believe it until he saw it. Many times before his beautiful sister had made plans to "go back for real." She was very bright and could have done well in college, but it never seemed her mind was determined enough to concentrate while she was actually in school. A few months after she "took a little break," she would say something to her mother like, "Well, I guess I'm going to the school tomorrow. I think registration starts soon." Her mother would of course be supportive, never really sure how sure Jeannine was about anything. "Yeah, they sent a paper here for you the other day. Did you see it?" she would ask her daughter. With that, Jeannine knew that her mother and father would once again pay her tuition and "get her started back in school."

"Good morning, Baby. I know you must be shocked. You don't ever sleep this late," Mama said jokingly.

"I guess that drive did me in after all. I was sleeping so hard I didn't even turn over. Now that's some good sleep." It didn't really shock him, though. He always slept solid as a rock in his parents' house. It wasn't the same house he and

Jeannine had grown up in, but just the fact that their parents called it home made it just that. It felt good. Real good.

"Did you hear me say somebody was here to see you? You better get on up from there."

"Who is it, Mama? I forgot how early folks come to call in the country." He let out a deep belly laugh that echoed in the room. His mother reminded him it seemed early to him only because he had just lay down.

"You get up and see who it is. I'm not your secretary, young man. But get yourself together before you come out and let folk see you. I think I can manage to hold her, I mean them, until you get yourself together. Get on up, now. She, I mean they, ain't go' wait all day." She laughed her sneaky laugh, as he and Jeannine called it. Whenever they heard it, they knew she knew something they didn't and she wasn't about to tell them what it was.

Among the many reasons she loved him, and perhaps because of this, was his scent. His smell. His essence. It was one of the silliest things she had ever thought of, but it was true. Marie loved the way ManMan smelled. Whether he has just gotten ready for a "date" and was standing on her doorstep. Or had just stepped off the basketball court where she was sitting on the sidelines watching him. ManMan always smelled good to

Marie. When they were young, whenever they were in one another's presence, all barriers were let down without much hesitation. In her mind, her spirit even, they had danced waltzes and serenaded one another on feet and with eyes lighter than the very clouds and as deep as the oceans God hollowed out before either of them were reconciled to their human forms.

That was before he left, though. She knew he had likely changed, and it frightened her. She was still staying in her Mama's house and often felt the pain of wanting the walls to swallow her. Mama was gone. She had no idea where her daddy was. And now it was just her and the memories, the essences. No, there were no children, although there had surely been lovers after she came back from Chicago. She had been lucky, or blessed, as her Mama would say: "You puttin' yourself out there, but who all you go' bring back?" So far, only the lovers — Charles, Ray, Detrick, Paul, James, and the beautiful Antoine — had come back with her. But ManMan predated and out lived all of them. They had never even slept together, but she remembered every touch, every kiss, every stumble, every hesitation, every nuance that invaded her then sixteen-year-old, now thirty-six-year-old body and soul. Her spirit had never been touched, caressed, soothed by the other men. That part of her, her spirit, was still waiting to be loved.

So when she heard about the death in his family, she tried not to get excited. She was sad for their loss, but hoped somewhere deep, deep inside her that ManMan would come home. She might not even get to see him, like the last time he had come home, but at least he would be there. At least he would be physically within reach. She had picked up the phone at least twice a day to call his father's house, but had not. She didn't want her excitement to come across as what it was. She imagined the conversation she would have with Mrs. Johnson, ManMan's mother:

"*Hello.*"

"*Hello, Mrs. Johnson, this is Marie.*"

"*Well, hey, Baby, how you doing? We ain't heard from you in a while. We miss you. When you go' come by to see us?*"

"*Well, I heard about your loss and wanted to call and see if you needed anything. You were so good to me when Mama passed.*"

"*Naw, Sugar, we alright. You know everybody from the church done brought more food than we'll be able to eat. We alright.*"

"*Oh, okay then. By the way, is ManMan coming home?*"

That simply would not do. She would just go

over to take some cake or pie or something. She would just have to go and see for herself. Not that she would get to see him or spend any time with him. She just wanted to know if he was coming. When Marie went to bed last night, she said her usual prayers: *Forgive me, Lord. Bless my family. Help me to live according to Your Word. I love You for Your faithfulness, and I thank You for Your grace. Amen.* Then her afterthought, unspoken prayer was "*and God, bless me to at least see ManMan if he comes home. I just want to see him again, Lord. Your Will be done, Amen.*" And she slept.

The 6:45 A.M. phone call could be none other than LaShawn. She was one of the very few people who could get a pleasant response from Marie that early in the morning.

"Hello."

"Hey, May, wake up, now. I'm on my way to work and I ain't got but a few minutes."

"You called me, Shawn, so don't be puttin' no restrictions on me this morning."

"Hush and listen. Guess who I saw, or whose car I saw at his mama's house last night, well, really this morning."

"I don't know." Even as she said it, Marie's heart immediately kicked into high gear like she had been running a marathon.

"Oh don't act crazy like you ain't think about

ManMan coming home for the funeral." LaShawn knew her better than anybody else and never failed to use that knowledge as the two-edged sword of love and conviction.

"For real, he came home? Did you see him or just his car?" She had other questions, but she didn't want to seem too anxious.

"Naw, I just saw his car, but I know it was his. Ain't nobody round here driving no new Jaguar." She hoped this would shock and please her friend, but, as usual, May acted nonchalant.

"Yeah, that's probably him." Marie slipped in a fake yawn and said before Shawn could answer, "And I thought you were on your way out the door."

"Okay, Miss Thang, I just wanted to let you know so you could get up and get yourself together. I been dreaming, girl, and I feel good about this! Arise and shine now, for your Light has come. Talk to you later. Bye."

Marie's head was reeling so fast until she didn't even say bye. She didn't hang up the phone until that incessant, off-the-hook tone began. "God, I thank You" was all she could think, but she was feeling something. Fear? Happiness? Anger? Or joy? Probably a combination of them all. Regardless of what she was feeling, she knew LaShawn was right. She was very glad to hear that Rayford was home again, and she did need to get up and get herself together. Whether or not she would work up the courage to actually go to the Johnson house, she wouldn't know until she was sitting there watching his mother go down the hall to get him out of bed.

By the time he got up, ManMan had figured that it might be one of his aunts or cousins or somebody. But the way his mama was acting, it had to be somebody a little more special than the homefolk he had grown up with. "Comb your hair and get yourself together before you come out. And hurry up, now. Come on!" And with that she laughed her laugh again, and pulled the door up as she left.

So he got up with a little more of a hurry. He went down the hall toward the bathroom, passing by his parents' bedroom. Daddy was sitting in his chair beside the bed pulling off his boots.

"Hey, there, Boy. When you get in here?" Speaking over his shoulder, Daddy sounded tired. He had just come in from the night shift and would probably be going back in a few hours. ManMan had told him he could retire any time he wanted to, knowing full well he would not. Daddy's response remained the same, "Well, I reckon I better keep working for a while, yet. I might get old if I stop." Then he would laugh and wink his eye at his wife, who would blush just like she did when they were courting teenagers.

"I got in late last night. I should have been up before now, but you know Mama cooked and I ate til I got tired last night. Then me and Nnine sat up talking."

"Yeah, I'm 'bout to go get into them peas and cornbread myself. Then I'm go' try to get me a nap in before I go back to the mill. But we'll get chance to talk while you here. I got some things I wanted you to help me see bout. We'll talk about it. You better go on, you know that girl in there waiting to see you."

"Okay, I'll be around here. I ain't going too far. What girl? Mama wouldn't tell me who was in there."

"Well if she didn't tell you, don't let me spoil the surprise." With that, Daddy disappeared into the bathroom.

CHAPTER 5

WHILE SHE WAS WAITING, MARIE thought about her mama. She guessed it was because Mrs. Johnson, ManMan's mama, was so much like her mother, too. She thought about the night she came back home. Things were so bad in Chicago, but she couldn't let her mother or anybody else from home know it. They had all, in one way or another, told her not to go. Not to marry Jerome. He was no good for her or anybody else. She was too young to be getting married anyway. She was just fifteen. And just because he had gotten her pregnant didn't mean she had to marry him and move away. They would all pitch in and take care of the baby. There was no reason to feel ashamed. Everybody made mistakes. "*Whatever you do,*" Marie's mother had said the day before her daughter left for Chicago, "*Don't get up there and feel like you got to stay. You'll always have a home here. If it ain't what you thought it would be, come home. If you can't come, I'll come get you. If I can't come, I'll send somebody for you. You can always come home.*"

And that's what she should have done long before she did. If she had, she might have been able to keep her baby. He was so beautiful and had the smile of an angel. She was always in awe of how he would look at her, straight into her soul, and make her feel so important. He had just started talking when the social workers came to get him. He looked at his mama over the strange woman's shoulder and said, "*Come, Mama. Come.*" He didn't cry, but he seemed to realize he wasn't coming back for a while. He seemed to know, too, that it was for his own good he was being taken away.

Jerome didn't come to the door. He didn't even look at the social workers while they explained that when they could tell "*a concerted effort was being made to improve conditions in the home, the child might be returned.*" Jerome didn't say a word. Just sat there in front of the T.V. flipping the channels with the remote, finally stopping on a basketball game. Marie was trying to listen, but the only thing she really heard was the word "home." What a silly thing to think at a time like that, when her child was being taken away, but the one thought in her head was the line from a play she had been in at summer camp. "*When I think of home, I think of a place where there's love overflowing . . .*" Then she heard the social worker calling her name, *"Do you understand, Mrs. Grayson? Did you hear what I said, Ma'am? . . ."*

"Marie. Marie." Mrs. Johnson was standing in front of her with a glass of orange juice.

"Oh, yes, ma'am. Thank you."

"He's up," Mrs. Johnson said, referring to ManMan, "But I don't know how long it's go' take for him to get at 'em. Here's some juice while you wait. I got some grits, eggs, bacon, and biscuits ready if you want some." "No, ma'am. I'm fine," Marie said hesitantly. Her mind had not come all the way back from Chicago, yet. If it had, she would have remembered that resistance to food in the Johnson house was futile.

"Child, I know you ain't had no good biscuits lately. And I put cheese in the grits, just like you and Rayford, Jr. like 'em. Come on here and eat a little bit. It's libel to be tomorrow before that child of mine get hisself together." She headed back into the kitchen, not waiting for another response from Marie – who knew what that meant and followed Mrs. Johnson to the kitchen.

"You know where everything is, Baby. Get two plates out of the shelf. I done already ate, so you and ManMan can eat til you get full. Rayford probably don't want none of this breakfast food. He'll get some of them peas and things I cooked last night.

So ya'll eat all you want." She was getting the biscuits out of the oven while she spoke, and took the lids off of the pot with the grits and the skillet with the eggs. She pulled the plate with the bacon on it out of the warmer.

Everything looked and smelled so good. Marie was glad Mrs. Johnson had insisted. She wasn't sure, though, how much she'd be able to eat. The thought of seeing ManMan again was making her stomach turn cartwheels. It was a combination of nervousness and anticipation. How would he look? It had been so long since she'd seen him. How would she look to him? She had tried not to make it obvious she was trying to look good, just short of Sunday morning best. Her hair had cooperated extremely well this morning, and the pastel pantsuit she wore was just the right mix between casually comfortable and slightly sexy.

"Let me go down here and get this man out of the bathroom, Baby. You'll be done ate and ready to go before he get out here." She went to the corner, and called, "ManMan!" No answer. So she headed down the hall. When she got to the bathroom door to knock, she heard the shower going. "Now I know this child ain't in the shower," she thought to herself. As if he had heard her thought, ManMan opened the door and said, "And no, ma'am, that's not me running the shower. It's Daddy in the other bathroom."

"I was just about to say I know you don't expect Marie to wait on you all day."

"Who did you say, Mama?"

"Well, the cat out the bag now. It's Marie. She come to see you."

"Did she say what she wanted?"

"I didn't ask her what she wanted. She came to see you, not me. So hurry up and come on down the hall so you can find out what she want for yourself."

ManMan could tell his mama wasn't going to come down the hall or call him anymore. Although he was a grown man with his own house, he still respected and obeyed his parents – especially in their house. So he said humbly, "I'm coming, Mama. I promise I'll be there in three minutes. I'm coming . . ." As he closed the door, he nervous system kicked into overdrive. He didn't know whether he was scared, mad, or what. The last time he had seen or spoken to Marie was when she told him she was indeed pregnant and was going to marry Jerome Grayson. He didn't remember what else she said, but he did remember what his response was. He stood up, looked Marie in the eye, and said, "*You been acting cheap all this time, you might as well marry cheap, too.*"

He remembered the tears she could no longer contain, and the sound of her crying as he walked away from her. His young, mannish pride would not let him admit it then, but he was more hurt than angry. His only response was to hurt back. He would not fight for her or try to convince her to stay. It was easier to let her go and cut his losses. He had his whole life ahead of him. She had chosen not to be a part of it. So be it. But now, standing there in his mama's bathroom, he regretted, like he had many times before, that he'd been so full of pride, so arrogant, and so afraid.

Marie was thankful for ManMan's slow preparation. The food was good to her soul, and Mrs. Johnson's conversation was comforting.

"Eat 'til you get full now. I'll just have to throw out what ya'll don't eat. You know Jeannine don't eat enough to keep a bird alive. And she'll swear she's full after two or three bites."

"Yes, Ma'am. These biscuits are so good, Mrs. Johnson. I haven't really had any good ones since Mama died. Ya'll must have had the same recipe," Marie said between bites.

"What you talking about, Child? You know your mama could make a biscuit that would float on air. And it taste so good 'til Martha White *herself* would be shame!" They both laughed loud and hard in agreement. It felt good to Marie. The laughter was like that she and her mama used to have when they were washing dishes or hanging out the clothes. She missed it.

Mrs. Johnson must have sensed it, and said, "May, we miss you around here. You should come more often and just visit. It don't never hurt to have a good laugh."

"I know. I miss laughing like this with Mama . . ."

"I know you do. Ain't a day go by that I don't want to pick up that phone and call her. You know how she would answer the phone: 'Hey there!' Just as loud and country as she could be. But we was a good match, cause I'm loud and country, too." They laughed again, then Mrs. Johnson continued. "But you know the one thing Sylvie always said, whenever she went home to be with the Lord, it would be fine. Cause life didn't owe her nothing. '*Gloria*,' she would say, '*You know I done lived enough for two or three people. And the Lord kept me through all of it. He waited in line til I got ready to come to Him — and He yet saved me. So naw, life don't owe me nothing, Child.*"

Marie was quiet for a few minutes. Her mama was the only person who ever really loved her unconditionally. Regardless of what she did or what mistakes she made, Mama was always there. Don't be mistaken, now. When it came to discipline,

Marie was well-acquainted with it. "*I don't care what you think or how you feel,*" her mama would tell her when she was growing up, "*You the child and I'm the mother. I'm responsible for you. So whether you like it or not, I'm go' do all I can to make sure you do right. I ain't trying to be your friend right now. I'm being your mother.*" Even though as a child she would get so mad she could have spit nails, as a woman, Marie knew that her mama was then and always did act out of love for her.

"Well, here come somebody down the hall," Mrs. Johnson said over her shoulder. "Which of these Johnson men it is, I don't know. It might be the one you waiting on or the one I'm waiting on."

"What you waiting on me for?" It was the elder Mr. Johnson's voice. "You got something for me? I sho' hope so. I'm hongry enough to eat a baby elephant. . . I see you still waiting, May. At least you got some good food to help you pass the time. . ."

"Yes, Sir, and it's good. Let ManMan take his time. This food is good!" Marie said it as honestly as she could. The food was better than good, but she was so anxious to see ManMan she could hardly sit down.

"He'll be down here in a minute I guess. He must want to look good for his guest." At this, Mr. Johnson laughed and sat down in the seat Mrs. Johnson had been sitting in. She was at the stove stirring the peas she had warmed from last night. "Them peas smell mighty good, *Mrs. Johnson.* I'm 'bout ready for some now."

"Alright, *Mr. Johnson*, I'm moving a fast as I can. Would you like cornbread with your meal? And what would you like to drink, Sir?" It amazed and delighted Marie that although they'd been married for more than thirty years, ManMan's parents always acted like they were newlyweds. He would say something to her, winking his eye or blowing her a kiss. She would blush and call him silly. Or he would be outside mowing the grass. She would take him a glass of water or tea. In her hand would be a towel and she'd wipe the sweat from his face. They would stand there talking for a few minutes, and the next thing you know, they would be holding hands walking across the field or down the road or sitting in the swing under the shade tree. She guessed it was the secret to their marriage: they always took time to talk to each other. And to listen to what the other had to say.

CHAPTER 6

"Good morning."

"Good morning, how are you?"

They didn't know whether to hug or shake hands or what. Both of them were so nervous until they could hardly look at each other, but something wouldn't allow them not to. ManMan thought to himself how absolutely beautiful Marie still looked. Her beauty had not diminished in the 20 years they had been apart. She was still the spitting image of her mother, whom anyone would say could have been a beauty queen. To Marie, ManMan was exquisite. His physical integrity, the muscles, the wide, strong shoulders were all still intact. But there was something else about him. He seemed to be shining. As she sat there watching him fix his plate, Marie kept saying to herself, "*Is he shining for real? My Lord, he is actually shining like Moses. My God, My God.*"

He was praying. What took him so long getting

ready to see her was not combing his hair or brushing his teeth. He was praying. ManMan knew he could not, would not face Marie without asking for God to – do something. He didn't know exactly what, but he needed something. So he turned to the only thing that had always worked for him: prayer. When he was in high school trying to decide which scholarship to accept, in grad school trying to deal with the racism he faced, or trying to figure out what to call his company, his spirit always led him to pray. He knew this meeting with Marie was just as important, perhaps ever more important, than any of those decisions. So he prayed.

God, I know You've brought me home for many reasons, most of which I don't even know, yet. And God, I bless You for letting me make it here safely. You let me find my family safe and well, and God, I Thank You. You know my heart, Father. You know the desires I can't even articulate. Your Word says we don't know how to pray like we ought to, but Your Holy Spirit makes intercession for us with groanings that cannot be uttered. Father, I don't know what to pray or ask you for about Marie. I don't know what I want to happen. I don't even know if I've forgiven her, yet. My spirit is anxious, but God, I want it to be anxious about the right thing. You know what You're doing to me and through me. I just want to be a blessing and a help, God. Don't let me hurt her again, like I did the last time I spoke to her.

If I can't be a help to her, Father, and her friend, move me out of her life again. I don't want to cause any pain, God. She's been through enough. And God, if You need me to help her, to be her friend, to listen to her cares, her concerns, her fears, her desires, I'll do that, God. Help me to forgive and forget what's behind, and God, help me to be a help to her as long as she needs me. I'm blessed, Father, and I know it. I want to give You thanks and be a blessing to others the same way You have blessed me. If You can use anything, Lord, use me. I bless Your Name, Jesus. I magnify You in the very depths of my soul. You are worthy, Lord. You are worthy. Cover me with Your Anointing so I'll say the right thing, do the right thing, be the right thing. I bless Your Name, Jesus . . . He took a deep breath, opened the door and went down the hall to the kitchen.

"Good morning."

"Good morning, how are you?"

"I'm fine, how have you been?"

"I've been doing really well. . . . It's been a few minutes, hasn't it?"

"Yes, it has. But one thing hasn't changed: I can still eat six of Mama's biscuits before anybody else can fix they plate and sit down at the table. I just don't dance no more." ManMan's comment eased the tension and made both of them laugh. It was an inside joke that ran between the two families. When he was little, ManMan would stand in the kitchen waiting for his mama to take the biscuits out of the oven. As soon as she would put them on the stove or the counter, he would grab one. For the next few minutes, he would dance around the kitchen saying how hot it was and still trying to eat it. By the time the rest of the food was ready and the other family members were at the table for the meal, ManMan would have eaten not less than a half dozen biscuits and would have three more on his plate.

When he finally made it down the hall to the kitchen, his mama and daddy had gone outside on the porch. It ran all the way around the house so they could look at their land from any direction they wished. Anyone who wanted some privacy could sit on the porch on one side of the house and never be bothered by anyone else coming or going disturbing their thoughts. The Johnsons had disappeared around the corner soon after they went out. When he finished eating, Mr. Johnson dropped a subtle hint to his wife of thirty-three years, "I'm going outside to sit on the porch if anybody want to come with me . . ." He nodded to Marie and told her to come visit more often, and headed out the door. Within a few seconds, Mrs. Johnson was making her way toward the door, leaving her apron hanging over the chair where ManMan now sat.

"You eating like you haven't had any good food

in years." Marie knew ManMan might be a little uneasy, so she, too, worked to break the tension.

"Now you know they can cook some exotic stuff in the city, but ain't nothing like Mama's cooking. I mean I can go out and buy the most expensive seven-course dinner, with cocktails and dessert included. But when it's all over, I'm sitting there saying to myself, 'I wonder if Mama cooked any greens today.'"

They both laughed and let a moment of silence stand between them. It had been 20 years since they had spoken or seen each other. When he got the cassette from Marie, ManMan hadn't responded. He wasn't ready to hear her voice or see her. That might have meant he would forgive her. Let her back in his life. Love her. Get hurt again. Things were going well and not even Anita Baker's golden voice or his sister's relaying all the things Marie had been through would make him risk feeling that kind of pain again. So Marie was surprised how easily they interacted. It had been so long and so much had gone on between them. Well, not really between them, but to them separately. It didn't seem like they should still be cordial to one another. Especially Rayford towards her, Marie thought to herself. How in this world or the next could she really expect him to let bygones be bygones and pick up anywhere near where they left off, where she left him? So she didn't wait for him to. She dove in headfirst and didn't worry about how deep it was.

"When did you get here? Yesterday?" Marie already knew the answer, but she couldn't stand the noisy silence that had fallen.

"Yeah. Well, it was really last night. Late. Everybody was in the bed. I was driving down the road, and it was dark in every house. Miss Annie Mae's, Uncle Charles'. Wasn't even no light on at BillBill's house. And I know he is always the last one to go to bed on the lane. I almost made it without having to stop and sleep. But when I got to Jackson, I couldn't go no further. My eyes got so heavy. I stopped at a gas station and slept about thirty minutes."

"I know how that can be. I get sleepy and tired trying to drive three hours to Montgomery. I can't even imagine trying nine straight. Why didn't you fly?"

"I started to, but I didn't know whether I'd be going right back after the funeral." He didn't know what his words would imply to Marie, so ManMan tried to clarify himself. "I think Daddy has some stuff he wants me to do while I'm here, so I don't know how long I'll have to stay. Probably no more than a week or so, but I just wasn't sure. After I drove about five hours, I wished I owned a piece of

Delta Airlines! I was some kind of tired and bored.
I forgot how ain't nothing but trees between rest
stops on the interstate. I rolled the window down.
Played some cds. Wore the scan button out on
the radio . . . . I finally got a little energy when I
heard *It's Been You All the Time.* You remember that
song?" He knew he was opening a door, and only
after doing so did he think about what might be on
the other side of it.

Marie looked across the table at him, and after
she finished the piece of bacon she was eating,
answered: "Yes, I remember it. And I know why I
remember it. Do you?"

"Yes, I remember."

"And?"

"And I don't know what else. When I got
that tape, I was surprised to say the least. I wasn't
expecting to hear from you. And then to find out
you were back at home. When Jeannine told me
what had happened, I thought about calling."

"Why didn't you?" She tried not to sound
accusing or harsh.

"To tell you the absolute truth, Marie, I was still
mad at you. You . . . it really hurt me when you
married Jerome."

"And that I got pregnant."

"Yeah, that too, to some extent. But then again,
I guess it didn't really matter to me that you were

pregnant. It was just that you didn't tell me first. I had to come and ask you about Jerome and the baby. I thought at least you would come to me with it."

"I didn't know how to tell you, Rayford." Tears welled up in Marie's eyes as she remembered when the doctor confirmed what the home pregnancy test had already indicated: she was pregnant.

"I don't know how you got yourself into this, Young Lady, but you are definitely going to have a baby. Do you want me to tell your mother, or do you want to tell her by yourself?" Dr. Ross tried not to sound disappointed, but he clearly was. He had been the family doctor since Marie could remember. Since her first shot "on her boo boo and it hurt real bad," as she had told her daddy. That's when he was still there most of the time. Not long after that he left for good.

"I'll tell her." Just as they had that day, tears were streaming down Marie's cheeks now. She had never felt like such a failure in her life up until that point. Her mother had such plans and dreams for her. They had become Marie's dreams, too. A baby was the last thing she needed – or wanted. She didn't even know if she loved Jerome. It was most likely she didn't. He was exciting and made her feel beautiful. ManMan was just a little boy in her mind. Jerome was just what she thought she needed. So despite the warnings from her mother,

from her friends, and from ManMan in his own subtle ways, she started dating him. Soon they were having sex. She really didn't even know when she actually got pregnant. It could have been the first time or the tenth. But too late to try to figure out or think about birth control or to just say no, she was pregnant with his baby.

ManMan got up to get some tissue for Marie. And for himself. He was crying with her. What he couldn't figure out was whether he was crying for her and what she had been through or for himself and how badly he had treated her. Guilt was heavy on him. *Father, help me confess this guilt and my wrong and let her forgive me.* ManMan prayed because he knew he'd been wrong and hadn't been a friend to her. Instead, he let his behind ride high on his shoulders and walked away from the person he had known longest, loved first, and loved deepest.

"I'm sorry," he tried to apologize to her and let her know she was still the girl he would gladly spend the rest of his life with, but he realized it would take more than those two words. He would have to do something. Make something better for her. Give her back something the whole ordeal with Jerome had taken from her. He would have to *do* something.

So he asked her quietly: "Can you forgive

me, Marie? What do you need me to do? Is there anything I *can* do?"

She was shocked at his questions and sat there for a moment in stunned silence. As she cleared her throat and looked at his still handsome, still sincere, still consoling and comforting face, she began to cry yet again. All these years she had waited for this day, for this conversation to take place, and now she was almost speechless and knew beyond the shadow of a doubt that she was still in love with him. Her heart had never moved from that love really. Regardless of what she had gone through with Jerome, she still loved the only man she had ever loved. And he was sitting there asking for her forgiveness. After she had walked away from him and married a sorry, good-for-nothing nothing, he was asking for her forgiveness.

"Rayford, what do I have to forgive you for? I was the one who left. I knew if I had stayed, pregnant and all, you would have still been with me. In my heart, I knew that. But I just couldn't make myself say I was wrong. I couldn't tell you or Mama or nobody else that I was a fool. And I knew it, too. When I told Jerome I was pregnant, do you know what he had the nerve to ask me? He looked away from me and asked, 'I know damn well you don't think I believe it's mine, do you?' I should have walked away from him then, but I didn't . . . and you know the rest of it, don't you? Did Jeannine tell you everything?"

"She told me most of it I guess, but if you want to tell me, I'll listen. Your version is likely more correct than the grapevine version she gave me."

By that time, ManMan's parents had come back into the house and were trying to pass by quietly. Marie took the opportunity to tell his mother how good breakfast was.

"Mrs. Johnson, you know you told me to come visit more often. I'll be back in about three hours with my clothes and stuff. I'm moving in so I can get some of this cooking everyday. Is that alright?"

"You know I cook everyday, three times a day without fail. If that don't happen, you know something is wrong. Come on and bring your stuff. I'll fix up a room for you."

Mr. Johnson couldn't resist and added, "Yeah, we got plenty good room, but you'll have to either wait 'til Rayford leave . . . or marry him one." With that he and his wife looked at each other and exchanged a sly smile as they went down the hall. They knew their son's heart and his love for Marie. She was a good girl, despite what life had thrown at her. Some of it her doing, some of it Jerome's, some of it just life's way of unfolding itself. But she was a good girl and the Johnsons knew it. They would be proud to have her as a daughter. But it had always been their conviction to never meddle in their children's lives. And for the most part, they didn't. A few subtle hints like the one they just slid into the conversation were about the extent of their input.

"I guess I should start at when we left for Chicago." Marie let a long, heavy sigh push through her lips as she reached for another napkin to wipe her face. Had she been crying when she was talking to Mr. and Mrs. Johnson? She couldn't remember and didn't really care.

ManMan knew telling the story again would be painful for her, so he reached out and touched her hand. "We don't have to do this now. I'm not going anywhere for a few days. We can talk about this later if you want to."

"No, if I don't do it now, I might not ever do it." And so she began telling him the whole story – some of which he had heard and much of which he had not. But it was all painful for him to hear, almost as painful as it was for her to tell.

"When we left for Chicago, Jerome told me to just forget about Mississippi. He would show me things in the city that would blow my mind. 'After you have the baby,' he said, 'we'll really get rolling then.' I asked him what he meant, but he just laughed. I didn't really think about it until after Kal'eal was born. He started acting crazy, always talking about how I needed to go to work and that he couldn't support us by himself. All while I was pregnant, he went to work everyday. Didn't complain. Brought his check home, showed me how much he made, and everything. When I wrote Mama or talked to her on the phone those first months and told her that everything was going good, it was true. He was the ideal husband and provided for my every want and need. I really thought it was going to be okay for us, for me and the baby.

"Then I had Kal'eal. Jerome came in when he was about six weeks old and told me it was time for me to go to work and that he had the perfect job for me. I told him I wasn't going to work until the baby was at least six months old. He said, 'You going to work tonight or you can get your ass out of here – you and the baby.' I went in the room and shut the door. I truly wasn't studying him. Next thing I know, he's knocking on the door. Or at least I thought it was him. But it wasn't. It was this guy he called Josie. He had come around the apartment before, but I didn't think they were close friends. And here he come knocking on my door and coming in the room before I could even answer.

"I was feeding the baby, and he said he would 'wait til I got through.' 'Wait for what?' He just looked at me and closed the door. Jerome came in the room and asked me what I said to Josie. 'What you mean what did I say? I didn't say nothing to him. I don't know him.' 'You go' get to know him, and I don't want to hear nothing else about it. I told you you was going to work tonight, didn't I?'

"I couldn't believe my ears, Rayford. Was this sorry bastard standing there suggesting what I thought he was suggesting? Surely not. He couldn't have been that big a fool. But sure enough, he sent Josie back in the room when he thought the baby was asleep. He came over to the bed and would venture to reach out his hand to touch me. I had plugged my curling irons up when Jerome left out of the room. I picked up the biggest one and stuck it in his hand. He hollered and here come Jerome. The baby woke up crying.

"Jerome hollering, 'What did you do? What did you do?' 'She burnt me, Man. She put that damn iron in my hand. She burnt me, Man. I thought you had it all together. I'm out of here. You call me when you get your bitch in line.' Josie left out still fussing and cursing like something crazy. Jerome standing there, pacing up and down the room, talking about, 'I know damn well you ain't burned that man. I know you didn't do that. I know you ain't that crazy.' I was so mad Rayford, I picked up the lamp and threw it at him. He didn't know it was coming, so it hit him right in the side of his head. And he hit the floor. It didn't knock him out, though. So when he got up, you know he was mad."

ManMan couldn't believe what he was hearing. Jeannine hadn't said anything about all of this. Then again, he guessed Marie likely hadn't even told her mother these things. If so, he was sure Jerome wouldn't have still been alive – in prison or not. Marie stopped and looked out the window for a long time. When she looked back at him, ManMan saw something in her eyes that had not been there before. It was like she had actually seen what she was telling him all over again. Finally, she spoke again.

"After that, he started beating me. Every time he thought about it. He beat me so bad one time, Rayford, I knew he had killed me. I couldn't see. I couldn't feel nothing. I thought I was dead. The only thing that brought me around was Kal'eal crying. I still couldn't see, my eyes were swollen shut. I got up and tried to find Kal'eal. When I got to him, he screamed even louder. He didn't know who or what I was. This girl named Tasha stayed across the hall and knew Jerome beat me. She came in when she heard Kal'eal and helped me. She told me to go to the doctor and the police. . . . But I didn't that time. . . ."

In the middle of another long silence, ManMan got up and put the dishes in the sink. He ran some water to wash them, but never really took his eyes off of Marie. When she thought she had gained a little more strength, she tried to speak again. But only more tears came. In what sounded to ManMan like a moan from the depth of her soul, she called Kal'eal's named. "Kal'eal. Kal'eal. Where are you, baby? Where are you?" She started crying again, heavily, and he went to her. Kneeling down in front of her chair, he took her hands in his and said, "Marie, I am so sorry you went through all of that pain. I am so sorry. . . ." Then he held her in his arms. And they cried together.

CHAPTER 7

IF HIS FATHER WASN'T UP early, ManMan knew something wasn't right. Even when he worked the late shift and came in at two or three in the morning, Mr. Johnson was always up early. This day was no exception. At what must have been five-thirty or six o'clock, ManMan heard his name.

"Rayford Telifero Johnson, Jr., if you go' live up to your name, you got to get up. The day go' get away from you, Son." His father wasn't in the room with him, but he had opened the door – and left it open – so ManMan could hear him. And hear he did. He couldn't remember what time he and Marie had come in from sitting on the porch. They washed and dried the dishes, she kept talking, and they went outside. Until it was dark, she talked and he listened. Sometimes she would ask him what he thought about something or stop to look at his face, trying to see what he was thinking or how he was feeling. But ManMan's face never really changed. He looked like he cared, and that was what she needed more than anything. So even after his mother prepared dinner and they had all eaten, she didn't leave.

"I don't want to wear out my welcome, Mrs. Johnson. I better get on back up to the house."

"Child, sit down here and you and ManMan shell these peas so I can cook 'em for dinner." In her most matriarchal voice, Mrs. Johnson both invited and insisted that she stay for dinner. So she stayed.

"Are you going to get up anytime this morning, Son? I sho' don't want to have to wait until tomorrow to take care of this little business I need you to help me with." Mr. Johnson knew how to ask a question and give you the answer at the same time.

ManMan dragged sleepily down the hall following the smell of coffee. His mother was already up rummaging around in the kitchen. She was ready to prepare breakfast. Jeannine was not in the kitchen. ManMan knew she wouldn't be. Regardless of how early her parents got up, it never phased Jeannine. "That gal could sleep through a tornado and never even turn over," Mr. Johnson always said.

"Daddy, I'm up. I didn't know you needed me to do anything this morning. You should have told me last night, and I would have been up and ready."

"That's alright. It ain't but five-thirty. You still got time to get ready. The courthouse don't open til eight. The bank don't open til nine. The lawyer won't get to his office before ten. You got time to get ready." Mr. Johnson was pouring his second cup of coffee as he talked to ManMan. By his third, he would be tired of it and let it sit in the cup until it was cold. But right now, cup number two was hot and piping and smelled good to ManMan. He didn't really want any, but he loved the smell of it.

"Do I need to take anything with me, Daddy? I brought those papers home you sent me last month . . ." His voice was stopped when Mr. Johnson, Sr. looked around at him. It was a "*Did I tell you to say anything about that*?" look. So ManMan hushed and did not finish the statement. Rather, he jumped to another. "Well, I'll go get ready and you let me know when it's time to go. I'll be ready." As he went down the hall, he heard his mother ask, "What papers he talking about, Baby?" There was no answer, and she didn't ask again.

What was that all about, Lord? I haven't ever known Daddy to keep anything from Mama. That was different . . . Just show me what I need to do. Bless me to be a blessing to my parents, my family, and to Marie. Especially Marie. Use me as the vessel to help bring her life back together. Wherever her child is, bless him. Even bless that sorry excuse for a man who called himself her husband. Forgive me, Father, but I can't say I need to see him in this life ever again . . . Whatever you need from me, God, I'll give it. Help me not be afraid to give all of myself when and where You see fit. I don't want to Love wrong, Father, for the wrong reasons or with the wrong motives. I want to be used by You, according to Your Holy and Divine Will. If you can use anything, Lord, You can use me. I bless and praise Your Name, God. I magnify Your Presence in my life. I give You glory and honor, for You alone are worthy . . ."

The ringing of the phone momentarily took ManMan's mind off of his prayer, and he listened as his mother's conversation indicated the call was for her. He took out the papers and read them again. All of the information was about the land, the house, a bank account, everything his father had accumulated over his fifty-seven years. Copies of deeds and records of insurance payments and policy specifics. A bank statement dated a little less than a two months ago indicating an account with a balance of almost $175,000.00. When he had gotten the packet of papers last summer, ManMan opened it quickly because he recognized his father's handwriting. As it had always been, it was a bit shakey, but readable none the less.

His thoughts were interrupted when his mother knocked on the door to his room. "You got a phone call. Here's the phone. Or you want me to take a message?"

"No, Ma'am, I'll take it." He opened the door to get the cordless phone from her, and she quietly closed the door as she left to go back toward the kitchen.

"Hello, this is Rayford."

"Hello, Mr. Johnson, this is Tracy. How is your vacation going, Sir?"

"It's going very well, Mr. Scott. How are things holding together there?" Tracy Scott had been with the company since its inception and was by far ManMan's most valuable employee. He had the company and its vision in his heart and fought fiercely against anyone or anything that came against it.

"Very well, Sir. I just called to give you an update on those two projects you asked me to keep you informed about."

"Yes, very good. Did Mr. Wrensford call to set up a time to see visit the Lakewood site?"

"Yes, Sir, he did. Ms. Davis took him to the site, and he was very pleased with the progress. His comment was, and I quote, 'I never in my wildest imagination expected it to be so magnificent. And it's not even finished yet.'"

"He was really impressed, huh?"

"Highly impressed, Sir."

"Good, good. That's good to hear. And what about Dr. Howard? Did she and her partners visit the medical complex?"

"Yes, Sir, they did. She had one concern about the height of the columns in front of the main building. She indicated that her desire was that they be taller than they are. But I let her know what she was seeing was not the finished height. Mr. Crawford took her into his office at the site and showed her how the top of the column is designed to integrate the initials of all the partners into one flowing design. She was so excited, Sir. Her partners teased her that she always knew how to spoil a surprise. But all and all, they were pleased. Dr. Howard asked if we were taking new projects at this time. I told her I would ask when I spoke to you."

"Well, I don't really know how long I'll be here, but set up a meeting and talk to her. See where she's heading. If it's something she's planning for the next few months, we can't do it. For the next year or so, it's very possible. For the next three years, it's definite. Just talk with her and let me know. Is there anything else? Has Mrs. Langston had the baby yet? Or babies, shall I say."

"No, Sir. She said she figures they're waiting for their boss to come back into town."

"Tell her she can let them know it's okay. They don't have to wait. I'll see them when I get back."

"Yes, Sir, I'll be sure to tell her."

"Well, is there anything else I need to be brought up to speed on?"

"No, Sir. Things are going very well. Is there anything specific you need any of us to do?"

"No, just do what you do best. I'll be calling in and you can call me as things develop. I have complete confidence in you all. God has blessed me with some Anointed, intelligent, highly-favored employees. Amen?"

"Yes, Sir, amen."

"Alright then. We'll talk in a couple of days."

"Yes, Sir. . . Mr. Johnson, I apologize, Sir. I almost forgot. You received a phone call from a Mr. Grayson, Jerome Grayson. The call was collect and I accepted it because I thought it might be you. . . Mr. Johnson? Are you there, Sir?"

"Yes, I'm here. *Who did you say?*"

"Grayson, Sir. Jerome Grayson."

"When did he call?"

"Yesterday at 1:32 P.M."

"And he wanted what? Where was he calling from?"

"He was actually calling from Illinois State Prison, Sir. And he didn't say what he wanted. Only that he needed to talk to you and asked if

I would make sure you got the message and the number where you can call him back."

"Okay."

"Would you like the number, Sir? I have it right here."

"No, just keep it until I get back."

"Are you alright, Mr. Johnson?Did I do something wrong? I only accepted the call because I thought it might be you."

"No, no, you didn't do anything wrong. . . I'll talk to you in a couple of days. If anything comes up, you can call me before then. Tell everyone I said hello."

"I will, Sir. Goodbye." "Goodbye."

"Tracy . . ."

"Yes, sir?"

"Give me that number."

ManMan could hardly comprehend what he had just heard. Jerome called his office looking for him? How in the name of Heaven had he gotten his number, and why would he call? It was truly a shock. And a mystery. *God, what is he calling me for? What does he want from me?*

CHAPTER 8

Marie left the Johnson's house very late. She imagined it was actually about two or three o'clock in the morning. But she felt better than she had in a long time. Talking to ManMan blessed her very soul, and she was so glad she'd gone to his parents' house. The same love she felt before she went to Chicago, the same warmth and honesty she heard in his mother's voice, the same strength and integrity she'd always seen in his father's character, all these things remained. They made her feel comfortable and she thanked God for that. Despite all the hardships she'd experienced, some of which life put on her and some of which she foolishly picked up herself, it was good to know that there was still a place where love was real, abundant, and unconditional.

The most blessed thing by far was Rayford. It was like they hadn't been apart at all, and all the things she told him about Chicago didn't seem to

affect him. Not that he acted unconcerned, because he was attentive and listened to every word she said. He seemed to hear and feel the things she couldn't even articulate. But none of it affected him in a way that would make him want to just wash his hands of her. He wasn't offended or shocked or judgmental. At times, he asked her if she was alright, reached out and touched her hand or her shoulder, got her water or tissue, and finally just held her hand and didn't let go. She felt so good being near him, and she was hopeful that they could build a solid relationship. She was even beginning to feel hopeful that she could find her son again.

She poured her story out to ManMan last night like it had been tearing her up and if she didn't find a safe place to tell it, she would be consumed from the inside out. When he didn't flinch or falter after she told him about the work Jerome planned for her to do, she kept pouring out. Things hadn't gotten any better, but had grown steadily worse after Josey came to the apartment and Jerome beat her for the first time. Everyday she would pray that she could keep the door locked or run fast enough or be quiet enough for him not to beat her. She promised herself after every beating she would call the police or leave or something. Kill him. Stab him. Something. But she never did.

All she could hear when she was at the point of

doing something to him was "*Thou shall not kill.*" Like the time she had put the poison in his food. He came in and she asked him if he was ready to eat. He said he would come when he got *damn* ready and not to ask him again. She didn't. She put the food on the plate and left it covered on the table for him. She went in the room and listened for him to come to the table. Still, she heard, *Thou shall not kill.* As much as she wanted him away from her and out of Kal'eal's life, as many times as he had beaten her to within an inch of her own life, she still heard the Words she knew were right. They had been taught to her when she and ManMan were children in church, and they were still a part of her.

So when Jerome got up off the couch and came to the table, she ran out of the room and knocked the plate off the table. Of course, he jumped up and hit her, knocking her on the floor in the same place the food had landed. "Bitch, what's wrong with you?" He kicked her in the stomach and stormed out of the door. She lay there wondering what was wrong with her. That was her perfect chance. He would have been gone before the night was over. It couldn't have been that she loved him. That, she realized shortly after they arrived in Chicago, had never been the case. She wasn't worried about how it would affect Kal'eal. He was afraid of Jerome and cried every time his father came near him. No matter how tender he tried to be and despite the fact that he'd never actually seen Jerome beat Marie, Kal'eal could see the evil in his father's heart.

Why did she never call the police or go for help? That was still a mystery to her. Jerome always told her that he had friends on the police force and that even if he went to jail, they would come and "get rid of her for him, and Kal'eal, too." It must have made an impact on her. The one time he did go to jail, not for anything he did to her but for drug possession, he was out before she even knew he had been in. One of the policemen had come to the door to ask for Jerome. Of course, he wasn't there. The cop had told her, "Well, when he gets here, tell him to stay here. They looking for him downtown." From that, Marie guessed that Jerome did have connections. By the time he got home that evening and she gave him the message, he said, "I done already been down there. Them punks can't do nothing to me. I told you – I know people."

After that, she didn't really think about calling the police. And leaving would have meant only one thing: going home to Mississippi. Right before the social workers came, she had almost decided that was what she was going to do. Take her son and go home to her mother. It would mean she'd have to admit to everybody back home that she'd been wrong, she shouldn't have married Jerome, he wasn't any good, and she had failed. It would be hard, but at that point, hard in Waynesboro, Mississippi, would be better than hell in Chicago, Illinois. She called the bus station and asked how much two one-way tickets home would be. Since Kal'eal was less than six years old, she wouldn't have to pay full price for him. He could have a seat beside her if the bus was not full, but if so, she might have to hold him. That was fine. The best time to leave would be in the afternoon when she knew Jerome would be out. He probably didn't care that she was leaving, but he wasn't going to be separated from his son unless he chose to be. The three o'clock bus would get them there late the next evening. Fine. As long as they got out of Chicago.

But the next morning, at 9:03 A.M., the knock on the door scared her. She thought Mark had gotten confused and come too early. He was actually Jerome's friend, and he drove a taxi. When Marie asked him, he had immediately agreed to help her get to the bus station and away from Jerome. "That mean bastard go' kill you if you don't get out of there. I'll help you. What time you want me to come?" She had said two o'clock. Why was he there so early? Another thought struck panic in her: maybe he was actually coming to tell Jerome of her plan. She was even more afraid when that thought crossed her mind.

As she went to open the door, Jerome asked, "Are you expecting somebody?" and laughed. She was sure Mark had told him then. All she could do was pray. *Lord, don't let this be Mark. Please, Lord, spare me from that.* The two women and one man who were at the door were worse than Mark. They stood there with solid faces and held out a paper toward Marie.

"Are you Mrs. Marie Grayson?" Marie nodded yes. "This is for you. You can take a moment to read it if you need to, but it is an order of protection for your son, Kal'eal Grayson. The document authorizes us to remove the child from this environment in order to insure his safety."

By this time, all three were in the house and the man was standing directly over Jerome, ready to use force if he had to. While the first woman continued to talk and give Marie identification for all three of them, the second woman went down the hall opening doors to the first bedroom and the bathroom looking for Kal'eal. Marie was so shocked until she couldn't even speak. A thousand questions were running through her mind – Who had called these people? Why did Kal'eal need an order of protection against her? Why hadn't they come before and given her some kind of warning or something? Why didn't she leave with Kal'eal early that morning? Why hadn't Jerome said anything? He just sat there flipping the channels on the television. His only remark was made to the man who was standing over him. "You ain't got to worry, Partner," he said coldly, "I ain't go' try to stop you. I ain't got nothing to do with it." Sooner than she could come to her senses and think rationally or get the questions to take shape and be verbalized, the women were gone with her son. He looked sadly over the woman's shoulder who had gone down the hall to find him and beckoned for his mother. "Come, Mama. Come." And then he was gone.

The next thing she knew, she was in her mother's arms, in her mother's house, laying on the floor crying. She remembered hearing her mother talking to someone, not her, but talking with fierce determination and even desperation. Later on she realized that her mother was actually praying. She couldn't remember to save her life, even now after all these years, how she had gotten home or to the bus station or on the bus or from the bus station to her mother's house when she got to Mississippi. All she knew – because her mother had told her – was that for three days she slept and did not eat or get up out of the bed except one time to go to the bathroom. It wasn't to use the bathroom, though. She began to vomit, and her mother thought she wouldn't ever stop. She held her child's hair and rubbed her back and prayed some more. *Father, heal my child. Get it all out of her, Father. Move by Your Spirit and heal my child. Only You can deliver her from this hell, Father. Strengthen her in her soul. Angels, I charge you to be on your duty. Stand guard around this child and fight the devil for her. She can't do it right now. Angels, be on your charge now. Fight for this child. In the Name of Jesus, do it now. And Marie, you be healed in your body in the Name of Jesus. Healed I say, By the stripes of Jesus and in His Name, you are healed!"* She immediately stopped vomiting and went back to bed.

Her mother told her later she hadn't really slept at all. She would lie down and bolt straight up in the bed reaching for something. "What is it," Mrs. Carter would ask, "What is it, Baby?" Marie wouldn't answer. Instead she would just stare into the nothingness in front of her and begin to cry. She would fold her arms close to her and begin to rock whatever she thought she was holding. Then she would lie down and try to sleep, only to bolt again. This continued for three days, and her mother didn't eat for three days. She wasn't worried, but she told God, *"If You need a sacrifice or repentance or confession, my child can't do it right now. So I'll do it for her."* That's exactly what she did, too. She slept in the same room with Marie and prayed for hours on end, even when Marie bolted and reached, especially then. But not one time did she get tired or lose her strength or her focus.

Every time the phone rang during the first day, she would just ignore it. After that, she turned the ringer off. She did call ManMan's mother, though. "I need you to get on your face before the Lord for this child, Gloria. She wrestling some demon and she need us to fight with her. Get on your face, Gloria. And don't quit praying 'til you see me or her." With that, Mrs. Johnson began to pray and seek God's Power and His favor for Marie. She called Sister Thompson and Deaconess Jefferson, prayer warriors she knew would not ask questions or speculate, nor cease praying until Heaven moved. She told her husband, who responded by telling her not to worry about cooking for however long it took to "send the devil's imps back to hell" because he would be fasting and praying, too.

On the fourth day, when Mrs. Carter heard Marie call her, she was already in the kitchen cooking. She knew in her spirit that God had intervened and her child would be alright. Marie tried to get up out of the bed and go to the kitchen, but she was too weak. So she called her mother and asked her to run her a tub of water. The water felt good to her. She didn't know where she had been in the spirit realm, and although she was weak and tired, she felt lighter and freer than she had since she left home. When she thought of Kal'eal as her mother helped her out of the tub, she began to cry again. "We've got to get him back, Mama. We got to do something to get my baby back. You'll help me, won't you, Mama?"

"The only thing that'll keep me from it will be death, Baby. We'll get your baby back." True to her word, she tried. But before she died, they had still not been successful.

All of this Marie told ManMan that first night they saw each other again. Kal'eal would be eleven now, she thought as she got ready to go to work. He was probably tall and very handsome. As sorry as Jerome had turned out to be, he was devastatingly handsome, about 6'4" and had shoulders broad and strong enough to help Atlas hold up the sky. His skin was flawless and the color of cocoa butter and chocolate mixed together. Yes, he was beautiful on the outside.

The phone rang and startled Marie. She moved quickly to look at the caller ID and saw "Johnson, Rayford." She hurried, realizing that it was probably ManMan.

"Hello."

"Good morning, Marie. How are you?"

"I'm fine, Rayford. How are you this morning?"

"I am very well. . . Are you getting ready to go

to work? I'm sorry I called you so early, but I need to tell you something."

A million things went through Marie's mind, but not once did she think it had to do with Jerome. Maybe ManMan had a serious relationship he felt obligated to tell her about. Maybe he was going to leave sooner than he planned. Maybe he had thought of all the things she told him last night and didn't want to go through the hassle.

"Okay, what is it? Do you need me to stop by the house on my way to work? Or do you need to come up here? I have a little while before I have to leave."

ManMan thought quickly about what would be best and said, "Yeah, I'll come up there. Can you give me about twenty minutes to get myself together? I'll be there by – what time is it now?"

"7:00."

"Okay, I'll be there by 7:30. Is that okay? Will that give you enough time to get to work without being late?"

"Yeah, I don't have to be there until 8:30. We don't open until nine."

"Okay, I'll see you in a little bit then."

"Okay. . . Rayford, what is it about? Is anything wrong?"

"I don't know, Marie. I don't know. I'll talk to you when I get there."

"Okay, bye."

"Bye."

Now, Lord, the best man I have ever known has come back into my life. I love him still and I know You know that. I'm just asking that whatever this is, You make it work out for the best. I don't know if You brought him back here to be anything special to me or just to help his family. But whatever the reason, just make it work out for the best and according to Your will. I want him to be my real husband, Father. I know I messed up the first time with Jerome and I have known other men since Jerome, but God I know You have already forgiven me and cleansed me of that. I know every sin is forgiven and You Love me for who I am. And I know Whose I am: Yours. I Love You and thank You for Your faithfulness, Your mercy and Your grace. You are worthy of all praise, Father. And whatever it is, in Jesus' Name, I know it has already worked out for my good and Your glory. Remove any doubt and fear, Father, and help my unbelief. You are the source of every good and perfect gift, Father, and I rest in Your will for my life and in Your promises, for they are yea and amen. I Love You, God. I glorify You in this appointed time and this appointed place. I realize my steps are ordered. I submit to Your will, not my will, but Thine be done. Strengthen me. Prepare me. Regulate my mind. Speak to my soul. Move in my spirit, by Your Spirit. I Love and Praise You, in Jesus' Name, Amen.

CHAPTER 9

As MANMAN CAME DOWN THE hall in his parents' house, he heard his mother and father talking in hushed tones. They weren't really whispering, it was just the way they talked to one another when the subject was serious – or intimate. He wondered if the conversation had stemmed from the papers he had mentioned. It wasn't his intention to speak on something he shouldn't have, because he didn't know he shouldn't have. He heard his father's voice.

"I didn't want to tell you because I know how you can worry 'bout stuff that's already handled. I know you woulda worried yourself to death about this."

"You right, Baby, you right. I'm glad you didn't tell me until you knew what was what. You do know now don't you?" his mother's voice asked cautiously.

"I know well enough. Can't nobody else *really*

know for you, can they?" He paused for a long minute. "Yeah, I know well enough."

"Did you tell Rayford, yet? Is that why he came on home?" His mother's voice almost faltered, like his father's had that day on the phone.

ManMan stopped in the hall to listen for his father's response. "Naw, he don't know yet. I want to wait a while. After the funeral, maybe I'll tell him then. Him and May seem to be doing good, and I don't want to spoil that for him. He'll know when it's time. The Lord'll give me the right chance to tell him."

"Yeah, he will." She leaned over to kiss him and then held his face in her hands like she often did. He looked at her and remembered why he had fallen in love with her. She was beautiful, yes. She was sweet and honest and kind, yes. She had the most open and giving heart anyone could have, yes. But what endeared her to him and made it impossible for him to even think of another woman for the past thirty-three years was her tender touch. With her hands, Mrs. Johnson could calm the most treacherous and dangerous storms of the soul. Whenever her children cried when they were babies, she had but to touch them and they were still and quiet. Her touch was healing. Her hands were love. So in as much as she knew he needed to be comforted at the moment, Mrs. Johnson held her husband and stilled the fear and uncertainty that was raging in his soul. This time, though, she prayed that not only would his spirit be calmed, but that the disease that was ravishing his body would be still, too.

As he turned the corner, ManMan deliberately made noise so his parents would know he was coming into the room. His mother didn't take her hands away all of a sudden, but, not wanting her son to be worried, gave her husband a sly smile and said, "I Love You, Old Man Johnson."

"I got your old man," he responded with a flirtatious laugh. "Alright, Son. You ready for the day?"

"Yes, Sir, I'm ready, but if you don't mind, can I have some sugar from your girlfriend?" He leaned down to kiss his mother good morning.

"You 'bout the only man I trust to do that, so go 'head." As serious as their conversation had been before they knew ManMan was in the hall, Mr. and Mrs. Johnson now seemed at ease and relaxed in his presence.

"I have to go down to Marie's before she goes to work, but I'll be back and ready to go in a little bit. We can go run those errands when I get back, okay, Daddy?"

"That's fine, Boy. I'll be here when you get back. I was just talking this morning. Ain't none of this that can't wait. You go on and do what you need to do to take care of Marie and help her, Son. She a good girl, just had some hard times, that's all. When life get hard, you never know what somebody might have to do. Help her if you can. Do what you can for her, what she ask you to do. You might not can fix it all, but you can do what you can do, and can't nobody but you do what God put you back in her life to do. You hear me, don't you?"

"Yes, Sir, I hear you. I'm going to do my best by God and by her." With that he felt the urge to embrace his father, but before he could do it, Mr. Johnson was up out of his seat moving to embrace his son. He held on to him for what felt like an eternity and with all the strength he had in his soul. He held on to him like he was holding on to life itself. When he let go, tears were streaming down his face. This was not like Daddy, ManMan thought to himself. Before he could say anything, though, his parents were headed down the hall to their room.

As he left the house on his way to Marie's, ManMan felt strange. It wasn't fear, but somewhere inside him, he knew that things were about to change in his life – and dramatically. Was it his father? Was it Marie? Jerome? He didn't know what it was, but something in his spirit told him to gird up and get ready. *Everything will be alright,* he heard a

Voice speak into his spirit. *Do that which I have called you to do in this and in every situation and I'll do the rest. It will be alright.* ManMan thought about what God told Joshua, *Be strong and of good courage.* "I'll do the best I can," he said out loud.

Marie was pouring coffee when she heard ManMan pull up outside. The purr of his Jaguar's engine was so quiet and sweet until she almost didn't hear it. She sat the coffee pot back in its cradle and headed toward the door. She wanted to open it before he got to it so he would know he was welcomed into her home – and her heart. He smiled as he got out of the car, seeing her standing there dressed for work in a pristine vanilla-colored linen suit with chocolate-colored suede pumps to match. She always did know how to do that, and that's what made him smile. Marie could go to the Goodwill store and buy clothes other folk had become tired of, add a few of her own personal touches, and put together an outfit that would put Donna Karen to shame. Of course now she had gotten her high school diploma and gone on to earn a degree in Accounting, she didn't have to shop at Goodwill, but her taste in clothes was still unparalleled.

"Good morning. Come on in."

"Thank you. How are you this morning?" He asked this question, but the one really on his mind concerned Jerome, and ManMan didn't know how Marie would react when she found out the man who had beat her and allowed his own son to be taken away had called the office.

"I'm fine, but I could use a couple more hours of sleep. I enjoyed talking to you last night, but I ain't as young as I used to be. Staying up all hours of the night . . ." She laughed, and he joined in. But Marie could tell the laugh was not whole-hearted. "Come on in the kitchen. Let me pour you some coffee. I know you probably won't drink it, but I remember you always did like the smell."

"No thanks, but I will have a seat at the table with you. I need to tell you something, Marie." He pulled her chair out and then sat down himself. "I got a phone call this morning. My office manger called me and . . ." He couldn't believe this was so difficult for him. Perhaps it was the way Marie had cried when she remembered her experiences with Jerome and the absence of Kal'eal. Maybe it was the way he himself had gotten so angry that if Jerome had walked up, he would have had no trouble beating him to within an inch of his life. Whatever the reason, Marie had to pull the rest of the conversation out of him.

"What was the call about?" She was calm, not imagining it was about Jerome.

"My office manager called me this morning,

and gave me a message. Someone had called looking for me, and . . . it was Jerome."

There was a long silence. Marie's countenance changed. She was visibly shaken, but she tried not to let Rayford see it. It wasn't his fault Jerome had called him. He couldn't have known about the terrible time she had with him. Jeannine had only told him the rough sketches of what she had heard through the grapevine. Rayford couldn't have known. So it was not his fault that the man she hated called his office.

She composed herself after an eternity and asked, "What did he want?" Her voice was almost cold.

"He didn't say."

"Did you get the number? Did you call him back?"

"Yes, I got the number, but I didn't call him back. I wanted to talk to you first."

Another long pause. *Lord, what is she thinking? Speak to my spirit, Father. I need You to speak right now, by Your Spirit.*

"I want you to call him, if you feel okay talking to him. I don't know what he wants . . . Will you call him . . . for me?" Her voice wasn't really asking, it was pleading, crying out for help. ManMan remembered what his father had just told him: *Do what you can, what she ask you to do.*

"Yes, I will. My office manager gave me the number this morning. You go to work, and I'll call to find out what he wants. And why he called me."

Marie cut him off, "No, I want to be there when you call him. I can't ask you to do that by yourself. I don't want to talk to him, but I won't ask you to do it by yourself."

"Okay, just let me call Mama and get the number. I was in such a hurry that I left it on the table by the bed."

As he went over to the phone, Marie's mind reeled. How and why was Jerome calling Rayford? Why now, when he was in Mississippi? What did he want? Somehow Jerome knew she and Rayford would be together. How in the world could he have known? *He didn't know, but I did. I know the plans that I have for you, plans for good and not for evil, to bring you an expected end, Daughter. He didn't know, but I did.*

Immediately, Marie's spirit calmed, her head cleared, and she walked confidently to where ManMan was standing. She took the pen and paper from his hand and waited for him to repeat the number as his mother read it to him. 683-555-3333. As she wrote, her hand began to shake, which ManMan noticed. He hung the phone up and looked at Marie. He wanted to hold her, to protect her, to make her safe from whatever this was that Jerome wanted. But he realized that he couldn't protect her, only be there for her, in the way she needed him to be and the way God had ordained him to be. As her friend, for right now, that's all he knew to be. So he stilled her shaking hand and said, "Marie, let's pray. Before we make this call, let's pray." And with their hands joined and their hearts connecting, they did:

Father, we come together to first say thank you for bringing us back together after so many years. We bless you for keeping us safe and well, God, through all that life has brought to pass. We bless your Name, God. We love you, and we thank you. Right now, we come asking for Your guidance. We don't know what to do or how to go forward. Show us what step to take next, Lord. Give us what we need to do and say. If this call is one we need to make, You go before us and make the way straight. If it's going to bring more pain and suffering, Father, show us that, too. Just move by Your Spirit, Father, and lead us. We admit that we don't know and that fear is trying to come in, but we know You have not given us a spirit of fear, but of love, power, and of a strong mind. You have already given us everything we need. You have already made to rough places smooth and the crooked places straight. You have already ordered our steps, Father. And right now, in the Name of Jesus, we give you glory and honor, dominion and power, for all You do and for who You are. We give up all the worry to You, God. All the fear, the doubt, the anxiety, the uneasiness, we cast it on you, for You said to cast our cares on You for You care for us. So Father, we put it in Your hands. We'll do that which You tell us to do. We trust and obey. In Jesus' Name, Amen.

CHAPTER 10

WITH ALL THAT WAS GOING on with Marie, ManMan had almost forgotten about the reason he had come home in the first place. The next day's service had been planned by his father's sisters, his aunts. Their aunt, his great aunt, had raised Rayford, Sr. and all of his siblings after their mother died at age forty-three. Their father had been in and out of their lives, so he wasn't to be trusted to raise children. Aunt Bessie had lived a long life. She was 93 on her last birthday. "Child, I'm so old, Moses say yes ma'am to me," she used to say whenever she celebrated her birthday. And celebrate she did. Each year she began calling her nieces and nephews three months in advance to make sure they would be home for the Big Party, as she would call it. The older she got, the bigger she wanted everything.

Last year, for her last birthday party before she died, Aunt Bessie called all of the area nursing homes and told them there was an "Elders Awareness

Meeting" for those who lived at their facility, but were still able to care for themselves. "I don't want no old coots at my party," she told ManMan's father. When the vans and cars arrived from the nursing homes, she greeted the residents at the door and said, "Ya'll ready to become aware? Well come on in here and I'll make you aware of how to have a party!" The staff members thought about taking their charges back to the nursing homes and personal care facilities, but they realized they would have more of a fight than they could handle. So about three hours later when the last guests were leaving, one of the staff members whispered in Aunt Bessie's ear, "You have these meetings every year, don't you? Why you just now inviting us?"

That's the kind of life and energy Aunt Bessie had and made sure all the children she raised had exposure to while they lived with her. Rayford, Sr. and all of his eleven brothers and sisters tried to keep that vivre in their homes and to pass it on to their children. As ManMan sat in the house after the funeral waiting for his mother and father to get there, he smiled as the memories flooded his mind. "This is good," he said out loud. "It's good to be home, God. I feel good in this place, and that's a good thing. Yes, this is good." He said it out loud and over and over again because something had been trying to creep into his spirit and cause him anxiety about being home, away from the office, dealing with Marie again, talking to Jerome for the first time in 20 years, and maybe even getting involved with finding Marie's child. But he knew God wasn't in the business of leading him wrong or putting him in situations that were not ultimately for his good. And this was surely not a situation ManMan could have ever planned for himself. Again, he heard himself saying, "This is good. Yes, Lord, this is good and very good."

Just then he heard his father's car pull into the garage. After a few minutes, his parents came in, his mother first. She stood at the door and held it until her husband came in, too. During the service, ManMan could tell that Aunt Bessie's death was hard for his daddy. He had tried to remain strong and solid in front of the rest of his siblings, but the funeral was almost too much for him. He had gone out when the eulogy was being given and didn't return. When the preacher finished saying all the good, true things about Aunt Bessie, ManMan's mother went out of the church. Soon after, ManMan and Jeannine followed her.

"Thank you, Baby, I got it," Rayford, Sr. said to his wife as he closed the door behind him. She reached for some plates of food he had in his hands. Without missing a beat, he looked at ManMan and said, "Don't go no where, Son, let me put these plates in the kitchen. Me and your Mama need to talk to you. You ain't got to go no where right this minute do you?"

"No, Sir. I'm good." His stomach began to churn like when he was a little boy and had gotten in trouble at school. He would come home after school and be so quiet and so good until his mother scarcely knew he was in the house. Then inevitably, the phone would ring. It was Mrs. Davis, his homeroom teacher, Mr. Batten, the principal, or somebody from the community whose child had told them everything that happened at school that day. He would hear his mother in the kitchen, and her response was always the same. After the formalities and pleasantries were out of the way, she got quiet. "Oh, is that right?" she asked. "No he didn't, Mr. Batten. Not my child. I know he didn't." Her words should have sounded harsh, but she kept the sweetest, almost apologetic voice, and said, "Well, you know we didn't raise him to be disrespectful. I'm so sorry for his behavior, and tonight he will be, too." There would be more pleasantries, like asking "Didn't you enjoy church Sunday?" or "Can I look for ya'll to be at the bake sale Saturday? Emma's pies are worth fighting over. Tell her she has to bring at least five or six." Then the conversation was over – until his father came home.

"Son, me and your Mama need to tell you some things. We need to talk to you." Sitting there as an adult stirred the same feelings in him. Although there would be no "you know betters" or "I expect more of you" or the ensuing punishments.

"Yes, Sir."

"I ain't go hem and haw or dance around it. I'll go straight for it. I went to the doctor a little bit ago, and he run all of them tests and things. He said he found something, some kind of cancer." Mrs. Johnson sat close to her husband and held his hand. She knew he needed her strength, although she could have used a little extra from somewhere herself. As Mr. Johnson continued to talk, her attention was divided between him and her only son. Mr. Johnson continued. "The tests he said indicated that the cancer didn't seem to be spreading and that surgery was my best option." He said the words just like the doctor had that Tuesday morning, with the same matter of fact tone and the same almost non-existent hope.

"Daddy, when did you find this out?" It was the only thing ManMan could think to say at that moment. In his mind were about fifteen thousand different questions and concerns, but he didn't want to alarm his father by not saying anything.

"Well, I went to the doctor about three months ago. I walked around and didn't tell nobody til now. I just told your Mama yesterday, when you mentioned them papers I sent you. I guess I thought if I didn't tell nobody, it wouldn't be true. So I'm telling ya'll now . . ." His voice trailed off and for the first time since he began speaking, tears welled in his eyes. He looked at his wife but didn't say anything.

Sensing her husband's heart, Mrs. Johnson asked, "You alright, Baby?" Her eyes were clear and she didn't falter once during the conversation. "It's okay. Just take your time. We're not going anywhere."

Before he began to speak again, Mr. Johnson wiped his eyes and looked straight at ManMan. "If anything happen to me, and this is what I really wanted to tell you, I want you to take care of your Mama and your sister. You ain't go' have to send them no money or nothing. The mortgage I took out on this house after you built it was paid off almost as fast as the loan was made. And the bank statement I sent you was just one of three more I'll give you before you leave. And you know my insurance will be coming to your Mama, too. Naw, they won't need no money from you."

After he was sure Mr. Johnson was taking a break and not simply catching his breath or collecting his emotions, ManMan said, "I know you wouldn't leave Mama and Jeannine without something to take care of them, Daddy. But we pray that we won't have to find out any time soon." In his spirit, he wanted to say something about God being able to heal and deliver, but he didn't. Why? As he looked back on the conversation later that evening, he realized that it was because he wasn't sure he really believed what he would be saying. Yes, he had faith. Yes, he knew God could do anything but fail. Yes, God had proven himself over and over again, but never with something this potentially devastating to the Johnson family. ManMan's faith was strong when it came to his business, when it came to the integrity and strength of the homes he designed and built, when it came to getting on airplanes and flying from the east coast to the west coast to Japan and South Africa, and even when it came to Marie and all of the new possibilities and dangers associated with building a relationship with her again. But this thing about his father was almost more than The Man of God was ready to handle.

The fear was back again, and this time with a vengeful tenacity. The same fear that was trying to plant itself in his spirit when he and Marie were getting ready to call Jerome. She had taken down the number and just sat there looking at it. She wasn't trembling anymore and didn't seem the least bit uneasy. She said softly, "Well, we might as well call him. Will you make the call, Rayford? I don't know if I can hold the phone when I hear his voice. And I don't want him to think that he still has the upper hand. . . After all these years."

"Hello. Yes, I'm trying to reach Jerome Grayson. He's an inmate there. . . No, I don't know his number, but . . . And . . . No, I don't know his . . . Can you hold just a moment?" ManMan looked at Marie, "Do you know his social?" She wrote it down on the paper and he read it to the person on the other end. After a few seconds, the voice informed ManMan that "the prisoner he wished to speak to was in the infirmary and can not be disturbed right now." "Well do you know when he will be able to take phone calls? . . . Can you ask the doctor? Is the doctor in the infirmary? This is an emergency. . . . Yes, it does concern his family." The line went silent as the voice said, "Hold one moment please."

While he was on hold, ManMan told Marie what the voice on the other end had said about Jerome being in the infirmary. She didn't look surprised or like she had even heard him. Her face was still blank. ManMan couldn't tell what was going on inside her, he couldn't feel anything from her. He was about to call her name to get her attention, but the voice came back on the line.

"Sir, are you still there? Are you still holding?"
"Yes, I am. I'm still here."

"I'm about to connect you to the infirmary. The doctor will speak to you and will determine if the inmate you wish to speak with is physically able to do so. Do you understand?"

"Yes."

"Hold while I transfer you please. If you are disconnected, please wait at least one hour before calling again."

With that, the line went silent and ManMan could hear the click of the call being transferred. He held the phone.

"Hello, this is Dr. Bishop. How may I help you?"

"Yes, we are trying to reach one of the inmates, Jerome Grayson. . . Yes, this is about his family, and it is important. . . . Well, what exactly is wrong with Mr. Grayson?"

"Sir, I'm not allowed to speak with you on that matter. He will have to share that with you himself if he wishes to do so. If you will hold for just a minute, I'll see if he's coherent enough to speak with you. Hold on, please."

Another period of silence. ManMan was still watching Marie but listening to what was happening on the other end of the phone. He heard the doctor calling Jerome's name, but he couldn't hear any response. He didn't know what to think or what to tell Marie, who had finally come alive and asked what the doctor was saying. "He says that Jerome is sleeping or something. He's trying to wake him," ManMan told Marie.

"Oh," she said. Then she was silent again.

"Sir, are you ready to speak with Jerome? He is awake now. Please try to limit your conversation, though. He needs as much rest as he can get right now." The doctor must have given the phone to Jerome. The rasp in his voice indicated he had been asleep, and the cough that interrupted his conversation indicated he was sick.

"Hello, who is this?" Jerome was mad that he had been awakened. Maybe he had forgotten his call to ManMan's office.

"Jerome, this is Rayford Johnson. You called my office looking for me. I was just returning your call to see what you wanted." When he actually began to talk to Jerome, Marie got up off the couch and began pacing. She crossed her arms, perhaps in an attempt to literally hold herself together. She had gained some peace when she heard God speak to her earlier, but that peace was fading very fast.

There was a silence on the other end of the phone, and ManMan didn't try to fill it from his end. He wanted to see what Jerome wanted and that's all. He didn't care about Jerome and was not going to pretend he did. Maybe it was wrong, but he had already told God that speaking to or seeing Jerome again in this life wasn't something he had to do. Many weeks later and after several visits and conversations with Jerome, some with Marie, some without her, ManMan would understand very well how important it is not to tell God what you don't want to do.

"Yeah, man. I called you. I wanted to talk to you. . . . I, ah, need to talk to you. Some things about the past and what happened . . . with me and Marie. . . . and the baby . . . about our son." He paused, waiting for ManMan to respond, but when he got no response, Jerome continued. "I don't know how to get in touch with Marie, and I don't really know if I want to. I know she probably don't want to talk to me. I just need to tell somebody what happened with the baby and maybe they'll tell her. . . . I know ya'll used to be tight and all that, so I told them to find out where you was . . . You know the internet, man. You can find out just about anything you want to . . ." Jerome began to cough violently and must have put the phone on the side of the bed or dropped it. The next thing ManMan heard was the loud crash of the phone hitting the floor and someone rushing to pick it up.

"Hello, Sir, are you there?" ManMan answered and asked what had happened. The voice on the other end, the same doctor who had been talking with him earlier, said that "Jerome is having an episode, so you will have to call back on tomorrow."

When he was about to hang up, Jerome must have stopped him. "Grayson, you need to take it easy. The best thing for you to do now is to get some rest. They can callback tomorrow." Jerome must have protested again because he was soon back on the phone.

"Man, this shit ain't nothing pretty, I'm telling you . . . ah man, I beg your pardon. I know you saved and all of that. I'm still trying to quit using all that . . ." he struggled to stifle a cough and ManMan heard him ask for some water. While he waited for Jerome to finish drinking, he looked around for Marie. She had left the room, he didn't know exactly when, but she was gone. "I'm trying to quit using all that foul language, man, I'm sorry about that." In the moment of silence that followed, ManMan couldn't help thinking to himself: *This ain't the Jerome I remember. Apologizing for something? This can't be the same Jerome.*

"Man, you still there? You ain't said nothing since I got on the phone."

ManMan tried to be as calm as he could, all the time thinking about where Marie had gone. "I'm still here. . . . Is there something you wanted me to tell Marie?"

"When was the last time you talked to her?"

"I don't really see where that's any of your

business. Do you have something you need me to tell her?"

"Okay, you're right. That's not my business. But there is something I need to get to her, a message. Can you get it to her?"

"Yeah, I can get in touch with her if I need to. What is it?"

Another coughing spell took control of the conversation, and this time the doctor wouldn't give Jerome the phone back. He did, however, relay a message to ManMan. "Hello, sir, are you still there?"

"Yes, I'm here."

"Jerome asked me to give you a message. He said it would make sense to you and that you could call him back tomorrow."

"What's the message?"

"He said he needs to tell Marie where Kal'eal is." ManMan heard a loud crash of the phone dropping again, but it wasn't on Jerome's end. He figured out where Marie had gone. She was in another room listening on the other extension. She heard the doctor mention Kal'eal's name and dropped the receiver. "Hello, sir, are you still there?"

"Yes, I'm here."

"Well that was the message. Jerome said you would understand and to call him back tomorrow. So that you won't have any problems getting through, call between 10:00 and 11:00 A.M. He's in the infirmary, so they will put you through anytime, but the lines won't be as busy during that time. The other inmates are out in the yard then. Just call and tell whoever answers the phone that Dr. Bishop told you to call. And of course, give them Jerome's name."

"Okay, I'll call back tomorrow."

"Thank you. Goodbye."

ManMan hung up the phone and turned to go look for Marie. He didn't know which room she was in, but as he went through her house, he heard her crying and followed the sound. She was in her bedroom sitting on the side of her bed, crying. She looked up at ManMan and tried to smile. She didn't say anything and he didn't really know what to do. He knew what he felt like doing, going to her, taking her in his arms and just holding her. But it was her bedroom, and he didn't want to cross any lines, even if it was innocent and even if she did seem to need that kind of comforting. He stood in the door and just looked at her.

"Will you come sit by me, Rayford? I'm not trying to do anything that's out of the way, but I just want you to hold me. If it's uncomfortable . . ." Before she finished the sentence, ManMan was on the bed beside her and she was in his arms again. With all that was in both of them, they wanted to go further. To kiss passionately. To lay beside one another. To make love. But they both also knew with all that was within them this was not the time for that. They were both way too vulnerable. There was a task ahead of them that needed to be carried out without the confusion and trying to figure out whether they were friends, more than friends, or what. So they just held each other. They sat on the side of the bed and held each other.

CHAPTER 11

For I know the thoughts I think toward you. Thoughts of good and not of evil, to give you an expected end. It will work in your favor. . . I sent you here to do this work, to do this thing. . . . Don't worry, all is well. For I know the thoughts I think toward you. I am in control . . . For I know the thoughts I think toward you . . .

The Man of God woke up feeling the Anointing in his room and all over him. Tears were streaming down his face, and he was praising God in his prayer language. The news his father had given him and talking to Jerome on the phone was a lot for him to handle. He hadn't realized just how much until he woke up from an afternoon nap, which, under regular circumstances, he never took. He was also thinking about Jeannine before he went to sleep, wondering how his little sister would take the news of their father's cancer. So in the dream that had awakened him, it was her voice speaking the

Word of God so powerfully. He sat up and looked at the clock. It was five thirty. Jeannine should be home by now. He needed to talk to her. He wanted to tell her. He didn't want his father to have to say it again. It had seemed so hard for him to say the second time, first to his wife, then to his son, now again to his daughter. ManMan wanted to spare him that at least. And he thought he could make it better for Jeannine by telling her using their special way of communicating. He would tell her.

As he got up out of the bed, he heard Jeannine in the hall passing his room and singing. *I've had heartaches like this before, and disappointments by the score. I claimed the victory at last: this too will pass . . . This too will pass.* ManMan wondered if she understood just what she was singing. And he wondered too, if it really would pass. The door to his room was cracked a little bit, so he called Jeannine's name. She called back, "What?"

"Come here for a minute."

She opened the door and jokingly answered, "Yassah, Massa." A silly smile was on her face, but when her eyes met ManMan's, she quickly realized that he was not in a joking mood. "What is it? What's wrong?"

"I just need to talk to you. To tell you something. You got a minute?"

"Yeah." Jeannine came in and sat on the side

of the bed. Her brother didn't know how to begin. How do you tell someone you love that someone you both love could be dying? He didn't even want to think about that, but it was in his mind already. He had not gone to med school, but he did know that the longer you wait with cancer, the more dangerous it could be. Why hadn't his father told them earlier? Why didn't he let the doctor do more tests and start some kind of treatment? Why did he always have to be stubborn about everything? Probably because he was scared . . .

"What do you need to tell me, ManMan, you act like you're scared or something? Whatever it is, just come on out and tell me. You know how I hate for things to drag out a long time, especially if it's bad. Just go on and tell me so I can have a fit and come on back." She laughed out loud and waited for him to, but again, he did not. He only smiled a faint and brief smile. Then he looked at her. Really he looked straight into her eyes. He could not find the words. He just couldn't say it. He felt the tears stinging his eyes and soon running down his cheeks. Jeannine didn't know what was wrong, but she began to cry too. She knew that if it was bad enough for her big brother to be crying, it was really bad. So she cried, too.

Through her tears, she begged her brother to tell her what was wrong. "ManMan, what is it? Is it something about you? Are you alright? Is it Mama or Daddy?" When she said "Daddy," ManMan looked in her eyes again. She knew that was it. She stopped crying and said, "It's Daddy, ain't it?" ManMan nodded his head, but he still couldn't find any voice to speak.

Jeannine kept the one-sided interrogation going. "Is he sick, ManMan? Is Daddy sick?" Again, he could only nod his head. "He sick real bad? Is he real sick?" Another nod was the only response he could give. The tears were flowing so fast and so heavy until he couldn't control them. Not that he needed to. He knew it was safe to cry with Jeannine or his mother or even Marie. He picked up a wash cloth that was laying on the nightstand and held it to his face. Maybe that would help stop the tears.

When he took the towel down and looked toward where Jeannine had been sitting, she wasn't there anymore. She was on the floor, face-down, with her hands outstretched. She was praying. ManMan didn't understand what she was saying because she was praying in tongues, but he felt the urgency of her prayer. She was crying and calling her earthly father's name out to her Heavenly Father. She would not be denied. She called on Him and prayed His promises back to Him. She lay there on her face fighting for her father's life. *God, in the Name of Jesus, You said that by the stripes of Jesus we are healed. Ay yadda bosiya ekateboshiya. Ey yekeda bosiya ya shonde bosiya ha yaboekaydema . . .*

Pretty soon both brother and sister were seeking God's face on behalf of their father. Their voices, their heavenly tongues blended in prayer and the sound of it must have shaken the foundation of Heaven itself. With all that was within them and from all that they knew God would and could do, they prayed that evening until well into the night. They did not stop to think whether their parents heard them, although they surely did. Mrs. Johnson stopped at the door when she woke up from a nap with Mr. Johnson. He was still laying across the bed, so he didn't hear his children praying yet. But their mother stood outside the door and almost went in to join them, but her spirit was moved not to do so. "This is something they need to do for their Daddy," she felt, "let them do it." So she went on into the kitchen and began preparing dinner.

When Mr. Johnson got up from his nap, he heard something. He couldn't quite tell what it was, so he just sat on the bed and listened for a minute. He heard somebody praying and thought it was the television. He figured his wife had gotten up and gone to watch T.D. Jakes or somebody. But the longer he listened, the more it didn't sound like the television. The more it sounded like someone was in the house praying that loud. He slipped his feet into his well-worn house shoes and started down the hall. When he got to the door of ManMan's room, he stopped and listened, too. He couldn't understand most of what was being cried out, but every now and then, he did hear his name or "Daddy" or "my earthly father."

Soon he figured out that his children were beseeching God on his behalf. His knees got weak, and he thought he would sink down right there in the hall. His wife must have sensed it or heard him start up the hall because right when he was about to fall under the awesome power of his children's love for him, she was there to catch him and help him down the hall to his chair in the living room. For a while they both just sat there, not really listening but hearing their children praying.

Mr. Johnson was overwhelmed again and started to cry. Mrs. Johnson had tears on her face, too, and they were the result of the pride and joy she felt. How many mothers could boast that her children spent hours in prayer, together, and in her house? How many children would lay aside the fear and anxiety about serious illness and all its prospects to seek God with the determination that her children were? Yes, she was concerned about her husband and wanted with all that was in her to see God heal him. Yes, she knew her children were scared. They all were. But more than from the fear of what might happen to her husband or the guarantee of what pain the living would suffer if her husband died, Mrs. Johnson was crying from the blessing she knew she was receiving at that moment. Hearing her children do what she and her husband had always told them to do in the time of trouble blessed her soul and strengthened her heart. She was crying because she was blessed.

Mr. Johnson rested his head on the back of the chair and articulated what they both knew already. "You know, Baby, if the Lord see fit to take me home today or tomorrow, I know I've lived a blessed life. Do you know how good it make me feel to hear them children praying like that? My soul is happy, Baby, happy . . ." His happiness again expressed itself in tears that choked his words.

"I know, Honey, I know." Mrs. Johnson knew she didn't need to say anything else. They felt the same thing and both knew regardless of how this cancer thing turned out, God had been good to them. He had been faithful and not one Promise had failed to come to pass. He had been faithful and good. Very good.

CHAPTER 12

IT WAS SO HARD FOR Marie to sleep the night after the first phone call. She woke up not less than three times crying and reaching for Kal'eal like she had when she first came home to Mississippi. Only this time her mama wasn't there to hold and comfort her. No one was there. Just her and Jesus. Mama always said, "As long as you got Jesus, Baby, you don't need nobody else." That was true, Marie supposed. But she longed to have someone there with her. And that someone was Rayford.

It had been almost a week since they had last spoken. Rayford left a message on her voicemail saying he would be "helping Daddy for the next few days." He had called again, but she was in the shower. And again when she was out walking. She didn't call him back, though. Her reasoning for not calling was that he had come back home for a funeral and been burdened with all of this extra stuff about her life. Why would he want to be with her again? He was single, living an unencumbered life, actually doing what he had gone to school for, so why in the world would he give up any part of that for her? Especially after she had been so stupid when they were young . . .

The phone rang again, and she knew it was Rayford. She didn't know how, but she knew it was him. This time she answered. His voice on the other end was comforting, and she was so glad he called at that moment. To keep her from going back down that road of regret and landing in a ditch of self-pity it would take her weeks to pray out of. She put on her best voice. She didn't want him to even think she was as upset and afraid as she really was. She couldn't scare him away – again.

"Good morning, how are you?" The early morning roughness of Rayford's voice sounded good to her. Nothing sexual or anything like that, or maybe it was. In any case she felt comforted to hear the solidness of his morning voice.

"I am well today, how are you, Rayford?"

"This is a good day, Marie. This is a good day. . . . Yesterday was rough, but today is good."

"How do you know? The day has hardly begun. But I guess you're speaking those things that are not as though they are . . . "

"You know it. The Word do say so . . ." He laughed and gave both of them an outlet. They both knew they needed to talk about calling Jerome again. But laughter was better to start the day.

"What are your plans for today? Do you have to work this weekend?"

"No. I worked everyday this week so I could have the weekend off."

"You have some special plans?"

"No. Nothing special at all. Just trying to clean up and do some laundry. And my car is filthy. I'll probably spend most of the day working around the house. What are you all doing today?"

"Well, Jeannine's taking Mama and Daddy to this show at the auditorium. They're using a soundtrack with her singing lead on most of the songs. She's so hyped about it. She didn't even sleep last night I don't think."

"Are you going with them?"

"I want to, but you know I can't show up downtown without a beautiful companion. Would you be interested in being my beautiful companion tonight?"

Marie felt like she was thirteen years old again, and Rayford was asking her for their first date – chaperoned by his parents, of course. The butterflies in her stomach felt the same. The smile on her face was just as genuine, just as innocent as then. And again, he had to ask two times.

"Well, will you be my devastatingly, strikingly, magnificently beautiful companion tonight?"

"Well since you so accurately described me, I guess I will. What time does it start?"

"At 7:00, but we plan to leave at about 5:00 so we can get something to eat before the show."

"Do you want me to come up there or will you pick me up?"

"Now you have just insulted me, my Mama, and my Daddy! What man worth anything would make his date drive to meet him? You do realize this is a date, don't you? Only it's just like when we were thirteen, my parents will be with us." Laughter poured from both ManMan and Marie.

That night was simply marvelous, and it moved the Johnson family and Marie beyond their most hopeful imaginings. The show Jeannine had recorded the vocals for was titled *Born Again*. It was the story of a family struggling to come to grips with the loss of a son to street violence. He left behind an unborn child his parents didn't know about and came back as a spirit to try to make things right. The moral of the story, at least to ManMan, was that regardless of what people do or how many mistakes they make, we are still responsible for loving them. Sometimes that love has to be given in spite of what the person has done, not necessarily because of what we expect them to do, and sometimes we wait too late to try to make things right.

He knew God was still talking to him. Before the show began, he had decided he would talk to Marie that night when he took her home. The truth would be the best for both of them. He would tell her he was not ready to become the catalyst for healing or reconciliation or whatever was about to happen between her and Jerome. He would explain to her that he just came home to see about his father and take care of some business. He had to go back to Atlanta and get back to the company he had created. Most of all, he would tell her that he still loved her and that he could not, would not put himself in the place to be hurt like he was when they were teenagers. She would just have to understand. He had things to handle: his father was sick. As the oldest and as his father's son, ManMan had to make sure everything was in order – just in case his father didn't make it. Marie would just have to understand.

But *Born Again* and his sister's real, powerful, Anointed singing made him understand something, too. He *had* to be there for Marie. And for Jerome. And for his father. God had been preparing him for such a time as this. Regardless of how scared he was, because that's really what he was feeling – fear. Fear that his father would not be okay. Fear that Marie would somehow forgive Jerome and become enchanted with him in his illness, especially if he told her where Kal'eal was, and perhaps "remember" that she still loved him. The Man of God was scared. His faith was being tested and he almost failed the test. But the play, something that most people would say was not even real, changed his mind, convicted his heart, and strengthened his spirit.

So when he took Marie home that night and she invited him in, he wondered if she would bring up Jerome and the phone conversation from a week earlier. They sat on the couch after Marie went to the kitchen and fixed them sweet tea and brought a slice of potato pie for ManMan. She wasn't sure what he would think, but it was one of her best attempts at duplicating her mother's recipe. She had begun making two of them right after she hung up with him that morning. It would bring back memories for him, she was sure, as it had for her.

"Oh don't tell me you remember that, too! Potato pie, Marie?"

"Yep, I remember that, too. Mama had just cooked the pie and took it out of the stove right before you walked me home. It was sitting on the stove just as innocent, and here you come . . ." She couldn't finish for the laughter.

"And here I come in there talking about, 'There

go some of your Mama's sweet potato pie. She must have made it just for us, Marie.' And before you could say not to cut it . . ."

"You had the knife and was laying into it. Mama must have heard the knife cutting because before you could get the pie out of the pan, she was standing at the door with her hands on her hips . . ."

"'*Rayford Telifero Johnson, Jr., I know you ain't standing here in my kitchen eating my pie I made for church tomorrow. I know in Jesus' Name you ain't doing that!*' She must have thought that calling on the Name of Jesus was gonna make me not be eating her Sunday pie, cause she said it again. '*No, in the Name of Jesus, you ain't doing that. And I know this daughter of mine ain't let you eat it either!*' I had never seen your Mama that mad, Marie."

"You know how she was about her Sunday church dinners. Between her and your Mama, the preacher never did go hungry. Do you remember how she made you stay up that night and help her in the kitchen while she made another pie?"

"What do you mean how she made *me* stay up? I believe you were up with us, ma'am."

"Oh yeah, I forgot about that . . ." They sat and remembered and laughed for a while. By the time they settled down, ManMan had gone through half of a pie and was working on the other half.

"You know, you almost have your mother's

recipe down pat. I think I'll need to have at least one more piece to tell you what you left out, though. It might take two."

"I made it for you. Go ahead and eat until you can tell me what's missing. Then I'll have to make you another one the right way. Is that alright?"

"That's good. Very good." As he cut another piece of pie, Marie went to the kitchen to get ManMan some more milk. Tea was good by itself, or with a good dinner of chicken and collard greens, but nothing went with sweet potato pie like good, cold milk. Silence hung in the air as he finished his final piece of dessert. It gave ManMan the opportunity to think about how he would broach the subject of Jerome and calling him back. Marie must have been thinking about the same thing because it was she who began the conversation.

"I've been thinking about Jerome since you talked to him last week. My mind has been reeling from what he said about Kal'eal. You know that's where my whole heart is, finding Kal'eal. I pray he's with a good family, and I wouldn't try to take him from that, but I do want to see him. See how beautiful he is. Hear how smart he is. Does that make any sense?"

"It makes a lot of sense. He's your child, your only child, and it wouldn't be natural if you didn't want to see him, if you didn't care about him." He took a deep breath and continued. "I guess this means that you want to talk to Jerome again and find out what he knows . . ."

"Yes, I do. But Rayford, I want you to know don't expect you to be in the middle of all this. You came home to see about your family for the funeral, not to get caught up in this confusion. I thank you for making the first call for me, for returning Jerome's call, but that's more than you had to do. I release you from this, Rayford. You have your own life, and you deserve to live it like you'd planned before . . ."

"Before what, Marie? Before I came home to a funeral that had nothing to do with you? Before God led me back home in time to be a real blessing to my Daddy? Before I walked down the hall and saw you sitting at my Mama's breakfast table? Before I realized my heart is still connected to yours? Before what, Marie? Before I came back home and saw the only woman I've ever loved again? Before I loved you? Well, that's impossible because I've always loved you."

When he embraced her, Marie was in shock. He still loved her, and he said so. His kiss that night was reminiscent of their kiss after that first date twenty years ago. But the passion of adulthood took the place of the unsteadiness and insecurity of teenage fumbling. The strength of his arms made Marie weak, and she desired him more than she ever had any man. She wanted him to follow her to her bedroom and make love with her, but she knew they couldn't. They both wanted it, but when the kiss was over, they could only smile at one another and continue the conversation.

This time ManMan spoke first. "To be honest with you, I had decided to do just that, to walk away and go back to Atlanta. I was going to just let it go, let you go. Again. But that show. It did something to me, Marie. And now I know I came back home at this particular time, for this particular season, for a reason. And whatever this is with Jerome, that's a part of it. Do you believe that?"

"I want to so bad I can hardly sleep at night. I want you to be a part of finding Kal'eal and seeing him again. And I don't know if I can talk to Jerome without calling him everything but a child of God. But I know he doesn't need that now. He sounded really sick. The way the doctor was talking, he is."

"He did sound pretty bad when he was coughing. I wonder what's wrong with him?"

Marie was quiet for a minute. When she did speak, she said everything in one long breath for fear she might not get it out if she paused at all. "He might have full blown AIDS by now because by the time I left him in Chicago, he was shooting up with junkies from one end of the city to the other.

I thank God we stopped having sex right after Kal'eal was born. If we hadn't, I probably would have had it, too. Yeah, that's probably what it is. He's probably got AIDS."

The matter-of-fact way she said it made ManMan stop and look at her. She didn't have any feeling in her voice, and that didn't shock him, especially after the way Jerome had treated her and Kal'eal. What did kind of catch him off guard was the fact that there were tears on her face. Maybe she didn't know they were there or where they were coming from because she didn't wipe them away or anything. He couldn't hear them in her voice, there was nothing there. She *sounded like* she couldn't have cared less what was wrong with Jerome or what would happen to him – just so long as he told her what he knew about Kal'eal. Her voice was empty, but her tearful eyes told a different story.

"Marie, do you realize you're crying?"

"What?'" she said as she wiped her face. "Oh, yeah. I was just thinking about Kal'eal. I just hope Jerome doesn't die before he decides to tell me where my child is." The coldness in her voice made ManMan worry about her. Before he could say anything, she continued. "You don't actually think he's just going to come out and tell me, do you? I don't care how sick he is or what's happened to him all these years, Jerome is still Jerome. I heard it in his voice. That same syrupy sweetness he used to use when he wanted something. Like what he had to offer was so good . . ."

"Marie, I know it's going to be hard, but you're going to have to forgive Jerome for the past, and let him know you've forgiven him." ManMan was shocked at his own words, especially since he hadn't yet figured out how to do what he was telling her she had to do. And Jerome hadn't really done anything to him to be forgiven for.

"What do you mean, I'm going to have to forgive him? Don't you mean he's going to have to ask for my forgiveness first? You can't possibly understand the hell that man put me through, and now you can sit here and say so calm and easy that I've got to forgive him?" Again Marie's anger shocked ManMan. He knew she still had a lot of hostility toward Jerome, but he didn't know just how deep seated it was until now. Marie didn't give him time to answer before she continued to pour out all the venom that had been bottled up in her since she left Chicago.

"I thought you were here to help me, Rayford. You come in here on your white horse of self-righteousness, telling me about forgiving a nigger who doesn't deserve the love I would give a dog, and you expect me to say, 'You right, Rayford, let's call Jerome up so I can tell him I forgive him.' Well it's not going to happen. The only thing I need to hear from Jerome is where my child is and the only thing I need to tell him is goodbye and good riddance. Can you understand that? Can you get that in your head? If you can, I think we'll have a much easier time communicating about this. If you can't, I don't know whether we need to or not."

The ultimatum was harsh and even the Man of God had trouble turning the other cheek this time. He didn't argue with Marie or even respond to her questions. He thought it was best to just leave. To go home and let her have some time and space to calm down. He wasn't exactly upset, but he had to be honest with himself during the short, 12-minute ride from Marie's house to his parents'. How could she blow up at him like that with no real provocation? He had decided to stay and try to help her find out where her child was. And now she was pushing him away? The more he thought about it, the more upset he became. Where did she get the nerve to raise her voice at him? How could she even fix her mouth and her emotions to yell at him? Without even thinking twice about it, he turned around in the middle of Sudie Jackson Drive and headed back to Marie's house.

She opened the door and seemed surprised to see him standing there. He didn't give her a chance to speak or to invite him in, he just began.

"I know you're angry at Jerome. I know he hurt you. I know you want to see your son again more than anything in this world. I know all of that. But I want you to know something, too. I'm here to help you. You didn't ask me, but God told me to help you. And I want to obey Him. I WILL OBEY HIM, ONE WAY OR THE OTHER. We just need to get one thing straight here and now: I am not your enemy. I didn't do anything to hurt you, did I? No I didn't. So the next time you're feeling angry and upset and just need to vent at somebody, you let me know in advance. Cause I can't be responsible for my reaction the next time you decide to yell at me, okay? Especially when I haven't done anything except try to help and to tell you the truth. Now if that's going to be a problem for you, we really do need to see if our communication should continue or stop here. I love you, Marie. Always have, always will. But my love for you will never keep me from telling you the truth, no matter how bad it might hurt."

He turned to leave and was almost to his car when he heard Marie call his name. "Rayford, I am sorry. I was wrong. Please don't go. Don't leave like this. I am so sorry." This time her tears were real and her voice was sincere. She almost let her anger at Jerome and her fear that she would never see Kal'eal again get the best of her. She almost turned her back on her best friend like she had done before. *Lord, let him forgive me this time, too.* No sooner than the request ended in her head and her spirit, ManMan turned around and came back on the porch. He put his arms around Marie and let her cry on his shoulder once again. In that moment, they had not argued or had a disagreement. She felt absolute forgiveness and safety in his arms, and she loved him for it.

CHAPTER 13

RAYFORD JOHNSON, SR. HAD BEEN waiting to see the doctor since 9:00 A.M. His Mondays usually started at the mill or in the yard or in the garage tinkering with the old car his wife had asked him time and time again to get rid of. She had even threatened to call the junk man and get whatever he would give her for the piece of junk that's been cluttering up the garage for five years. She never had though, and most mornings when he was not at work, Mr. Johnson could be found working on it, always sure that the next turn of the wrench would be just the thing to get it started. But this morning was different. He sat beside his wife in the waiting room of the doctor's office, not really afraid, but definitely concerned.

He had almost decided not to go back to the doctor. He had definitely decided not to begin the treatments for the cancer. He had seen what they did to people. Every time someone would begin them, it wouldn't be long before they were feeling and looking worse than they had before the treatments. They were sicker than they were before, and they always seemed to die quicker than they would have if they had not gone through the chemotherapy. So he had decided not to go through that. If there was something else the doctor could suggest or offer, he would listen. But he was not going to take the treatments. He would give the doctor one more chance, though. Maybe there had been a mistake in reading the tests or something. Maybe he had read the reports wrong. Maybe. Maybe.

The nurse came to the door and called the person who had been sitting there longer than the Johnsons had. Mr. Johnson knew he would probably be called next.

"Well, they ought to be calling me pretty soon. I'm getting tired of sitting here in any case."

"You know how it is when you just come in without making an appointment. You just have to sit here 'til they get through everybody else. It hasn't been that long, just about thirty minutes."

"Is that all? Seem like it's been at least a hour. Did you see Rayford this morning before we left?"

"No, I didn't. He wasn't at the house last night when I went to sleep. He came from church and went to Marie's I think. After that, I don't know what happened."

"You ain't got to know what happened. But it don't take much to figure it out, though. She a woman, and he a man. He a minister, but he a man first. It don't take much to figure out what happened . . ."

"Get your mind out of the gutter, Old Man. You need to be ashamed of yourself."

"Ain't no shame in my game, Sweetheart. You know me . . ."

"Johnson, Rayford Johnson." The nurse broke up their flirting session, and her voice snapped both husband and wife back into the reality of their visit. She held the door and smiled warmly while they came. They must learn that in school, Mr. Johnson thought, seems like they all smile like that when they call your name. His name being called really didn't mean he was about to see the doctor, he knew that from experience. Even when he did have an appointment, the first time your name was called just meant you traded a large waiting room for a small waiting area. The nurse would call your name and then lead you to a row of seats in the smaller waiting area. She would then come and take you to a little side area where she'd take your blood pressure, then ask you to step on a scale, and, most of the time for Mr. Johnson, draw some blood from his arm. Until here lately, it was so seldom that he went to the doctor, blood tests were ordered every time.

"How are you feeling today, Mr. Johnson?" Her voice was warm and genuine. This was the nurse he liked. The other one was a little too syrupy sweet to him. She may have been just as sincere, but the little whining in her voice said she probably wasn't, or at least that she had something else on her mind and was just going through the motions.

"I'm feeling real good today. How you doing?"

"Oh we're doing just fine, too. Been swamped with visitors today, but that's what we're here for, isn't it?" Her shoes were so white, Mrs. Johnson thought to herself. They must be new. But then again every nurse she knew always had the whitest shoes. They must be made of some kind of special material that doesn't stain or smudge or scuff. She knew they had to get stepped on or blood dropped on them or something. They couldn't be that careful in a busy doctor's office or a hospital. Whatever it was, her shoes were perfect, not a mark on them.

"Mrs. Johnson, you're looking beautiful as always. I usually don't see you here with Mr. Johnson, though. I guess you had to make sure he came today, huh?" She laughed a little uneasy laugh. She was trying to let them know she was concerned about Mr. Johnson, too. He always made the day more interesting when he came in the office. His warm smile made the worst day seem more endurable. None of the nurses wanted him to leave, and even Dr. Barrette looked forward to talking with Mr. Johnson. Sometimes the doctor needed his visits, his conversation and his advice more than the patient needed medical care.

"Thank you, Daughter. You all always make me feel so welcome, I decided to sneak in a visit with Rayford. So it's really for selfish reasons I'm here." The three of them laughed as the nurse pointed to a seat for Mrs. Johnson. She took Mr. Johnson around the corner to take his blood pressure and weight, which was down almost twenty pounds since his weigh in only two months ago. He was losing weight too fast, Nurse Howard observed to herself. She wondered if he was eating enough, but then she realized that a diagnosis of cancer could affect every area of life, even if there weren't any real signs of the disease yet. Appetite, for food and for life, sometimes decreased due to depression. Activity often decreased for fear of injury or somehow speeding the spread of the disease through the body. There were so many things. She would make a special note to Dr. Barrette concerning the weight loss, and try to casually encourage Mr. Johnson to eat more. Although she couldn't officially talk with Mrs. Johnson about it, she would try to find a way to get the message to her, too.

"Mr. Johnson, what have you been eating lately? I know Mrs. Johnson been cooking some good Sunday dinners for you."

"Well, I ain't been eating too much here lately. Just seem like I ain't got as much appetite as I used to have. My wife still cook the best meals, three times a day mind you, but I just don't seem to be able to eat as much."

"Yes, Sir, I can tell. You have lost almost twenty pounds in two months. You need to bottle your secret up and put it on the market. Folks like me would love to be able to do that." Again, she tried to make light of the very serious issue of such a drastic weight loss in such a short time.

"Aw, you don't need to lose no weight. If you do, they'll have to tie you down to keep you from blowing away." They laughed as she ushered him back to where Mrs. Johnson was sitting. She told him the doctor would be with him shortly and asked if they needed anything. They said no, and Nurse Howard disappeared around the corner again.

"She said I done lost almost twenty pounds in two months."

"I knew that when you put those pants on for church yesterday. They used to be kind of snug around your waist, but you had to tighten your belt yesterday, didn't you?"

"Yeah, but I didn't know it was no twenty pounds worth of tightening. I'm go' have to start eating more I guess. I don't want to get sick on my own. That cancer probably go' do a good job at that . . ." His voice trailed off like it did every time he tried to talk about the sickness or even say the word "cancer." He believed every time he said it, he gave it more power. So he didn't say it too often and never too loudly.

He thought about how much he used to enjoy eating his wife's cooking. Whatever she put on the table – fried chicken, peas and neckbones, collards, cornbread, baked fish, fried fish on Fridays, baked pork chops, smothered turkey wings, string beans, mashed potatoes, that new pasta salad stuff – just whatever it was, he liked it. It was always good and she never had to ask if he wanted seconds, or sometimes thirds. He had always been a good eater. In spite of that fact, he had only gained about fifteen pounds in all the years they had been married. He was always active, doing something around the house, fixing something, or going to help somebody else fix something at their house. And he wasn't saying the quality of his wife's cooking had decreased, it was just that somehow he couldn't think about eating or food anymore. This disease was already trying to take over his mind and his life. He was trying to find the determination to fight it. He prayed that the doctor would have some good news. That was just what he needed to fight this thing. To overcome the fear that was threatening to strangle him, his joy, and his life.

Nurse Howard came back quicker than he thought she would. The doctor must have had a break or something. Or else they would just exchange the smaller waiting area for an actual examination room and sit there for a while. Again to his surprise, the doctor walked in with them. His "bedside manner," as they call it, was the best Mr. Johnson had ever experienced. Dr. Barrette was a Black man, like him, and he was young and really seemed to care about his patients. He often sat and talked with Mr. Johnson like he was the patient, not the other way around. There conversations were very comfortable, and Dr. Barrette always said "Yes, Sir" and "No, Sir" to his elder. The day he told Mr. Johnson about the cancer was harder than anything he had ever done.

He was quiet that day, and Mr. Johnson knew something was wrong. "Hey there, Doc, you mighty heavy today. Is something wrong?" Mr. Johnson had tried to lighten the mood. He wasn't expecting what he was about to hear. This was just a check-up. He had been feeling fine.

"Well, Sir, I know you're just here for a

check–up, but do you remember those blood tests we ran last week?"

"Yeah, you told me to come in last week to get my blood work done. Is that when you're talking about?"

"Yes, Sir, that's it . . ."

"Well Doc, what is it? Come on now. You know we always deal straight with each other. Whatever it is, just put it out there and we'll have to see how we go' handle it. Ain't that what we agreed on?"

"Yes, Mr. Johnson, that's what we always said . . . The tests indicated that there may be something . . . there may be a cancer . . . I'll have to do other tests to be sure, but the blood tests indicate something abnormal . . ." A moment of silence stood between them. They were both trying to find a way to apologize to the other. Mr. Johnson for getting an illness this serious, and Dr. Barrette for being the one to diagnose it.

That had been three months ago, and since then they had had several conversations about the cancer. He had come to the doctor by himself during those months, but since he had told his wife now, he asked her to come with him this time. As quiet as it was kept, she was his strength. He had always worked to put food on the table, but she was his strength. After God, she was the one part of his reality that Rayford Johnson, Sr. could always depend on. And he loved her with all his heart and soul for that constancy. Today, she didn't push him or pity him or try to hold his hand like he was a child. When they went into the exam room, though, he found himself reaching out for hers.

"Mr. and Mrs. Johnson, how are you doing today? It's good to see you both. I wish it was under other circumstances, but it's good to see you none the less."

Mr. Johnson reached out his free hand and responded in his usual manner, "Well, Doc, it's always good to see you, but let's meet at my place next time, okay?" A nervous laugh filled the small room as Dr. Barrette sat down opposite his patient.

"How are you feeling, Mr. Johnson? Is there anything in particular you need to tell me?"

"Well, Doc, I been doing alright. I feel okay most days, just a little sore sometimes. And I been sort of tired lately. The nurse told me I done lost twenty pounds, so I guess my appetite ain't what it used to be."

"Yes, Sir, I see the weight loss. Are you just not hungry or does food taste different to you?"

"Well, now that you ask, things don't seem like they have much taste to them. And I know my wife can cook. Everybody know that, so I know the food taste good, but like you said, I just can't taste it no more."

"That's one of the side-effects of the medicine I gave you last month. Are there any other side effects? Has anything else changed? Anything at all, no matter how minor it may seem."

"I can't think of anything, can you, Baby?" He gave way for Mrs. Johnson to speak because she knew him better than he knew himself in most cases.

"No, just that you get up more at night to go to the bathroom. I did notice that starting a while back." Mr. Johnson agreed with her. He had forgotten that.

Dr. Barrette made notes on his chart and shook his head indicating that he understood. "I can give you some more medicine to take care of the loss of appetite and the increased urination. Then you can sleep through the night and maybe pick some of the weight back up . . ." He was about to continue talking about more medicine, but Mr. Johnson stopped him. He put his hand on top of Dr. Barrette's to stop it from writing the prescription on the pad.

"Doc, I know you're trying to help me and you doing the best you can, but if you give me some medicine to stop the side effects from the medicine that I'm already taking, what's go' stop me from needing some more medicine to stop the new side effects?" The question shocked the doctor, but he had to smile at the uncomplicated wisdom of a man who could be dying. That fact didn't seem to phase Mr. Johnson. He was trying to teach Dr. Barrette a basic truth like a father would his son. Dr. Barrette was moved and understood even more clearly why he always looked forward to talking with this patient.

"Well, Mr. Johnson, you bring up a valid point. The other medicine might also cause side effects. To be quite honest with you, there may be nothing I can do to keep some side effects from showing up."

"I know, Son. You're doing what you know to do, and I thank you for it. But I need to talk to you about the other thing you mentioned last time, the therapy."

"The chemotherapy?"

"Yeah, that's what I'm talking about. Doc, I don't think I'm go' do that."

"What do you mean, Mr. Johnson? We already discussed this and you know that at some point chemotherapy will be required. It's the only way to really handle a cancer of this type. You do understand that, don't you?"

"Now we been talking all these years since you came here to work. Have you ever known me to be hard to understand, Doc? Of course I understand. But I need you to understand, too. If this cancer is go' take me away from here, I want to be able to enjoy the time I have left . . ."

"But Mr. Johnson, the chemotherapy might help prolong your life. It will give you more time to live . . ."

"What kind of life you talking about? Being sick all the time? Having to come here to see you every other day? Now Doc, I like you, but I don't like you that much." Mr. Johnson tried to ease the harshness of his questions. He knew Dr. Barrette was just trying to do all he could to save his life. But the kind of saving he was offering was of no interest to Mr. Johnson. As hard as it may be sounding, he was not interested in being sicker than he had to be while he was trying to get well. When Dr. Barrette didn't respond, probably still in shock, Mr. Johnson kept stating his case.

"I have seen what that chemo does to a body. You remember Johnny Davis? He was your patient, too. He told me about you. I saw him go from being able to work a twelve hour shift, get two hours of sleep and be right back for another one, to not being able to walk up two steps without having to sit down and rest. I don't want that, Doc. My life is more than that. If I get where I can't do nothing or can't go to work or whatever, I'll just try to handle it the best way I can. But I can't be taking all of this medicine and getting all them chemicals shot through my body. As long as the Lord see fit to let me live, I'll be grateful to Him. If He see fit to heal me all together, I'll be glad for that, too. But no chemo. No, Sir, I won't do that."

CHAPTER 14

THE ONLY WAY SHE KNEW it was all real was by the dreams she was having. When Marie thought about it, it seemed crazy that her dreams let her know what was going on in reality. The night after she had raised her voice at ManMan, as he had said, she had one of the most vivid dreams she ever remembered. She and ManMan were sitting on one side of a courtroom and Jerome was sitting on the other. There were a lot of people sitting in the gallery where spectators sit, and when she looked out, she recognized a few of them: her mother, her father as she remembered him from before he left home when she was about five, Jeannine, Mr. and Mrs. Johnson, Antoine, whom she used to date, and she thought she remembered seeing Mr. Batton, the principle of their junior high school being there, too.

At first the courtroom was very quiet. The judge had his back turned to the courtroom.

Jerome was very quiet, too, and she was moving her mouth, but she couldn't hear any sound coming out. ManMan was praying in his prayer language at first. Then he began to pray in English, calling her name as Marie kept trying to say something. Then the judge turned to face the courtroom. It was Kal'eal. Marie couldn't see his face, although she kept trying throughout the rest of the dream, but she still knew it was her child.

All of a sudden Kal'eal asked Marie what she was trying to say. "I don't understand what you're saying, Mrs. Grayson, or shall I say the former Mrs. Grayson. What are you trying to say? Speak so we can hear you!" He was mean. His spirit was cold, and his insistence that she speak only made her more inarticulate. She was soon on her knees in front of the bench, pleading for forgiveness. Jerome was saying something. What was it? What was he saying?

"Forgive you? Forgive you? How do you expect him to forgive you? You let them take him. It's your fault. It's your fault." Jerome was as mean as he had ever been. ManMan was still praying, only now it was louder and stronger. The more Jerome talked and condemned Marie, the more ManMan prayed on her behalf. She stayed in front of the bench, and Kal'eal turned his back on her. He didn't turn around any more, but Jerome did stop accusing her.

He came from the other side of the courtroom and joined her on the floor in front of the bench. He touched her back and said, "I'm sorry . . ."

That's when Marie woke up. She was in a cold sweat, and tears were on her face. It was these dreams that kept her from allowing ManMan to call Jerome again. Three weeks had passed and every time she talked to ManMan, Marie came up with another reason not to make the call. He didn't push her, though. The Man of God knew that if anything positive was to come out of their interaction, Marie had to be ready to deal with Jerome. She had to be ready to hear his voice again. She had to be ready to consider the possibility of forgiving him. If she wasn't ready yet, she just wasn't ready.

Her call in the middle of the day surprised him. He was on the phone with his office in Atlanta and would have ignored the call waiting beep if he hadn't seen her number on the caller id. He said goodbye to his office manager and clicked over to talk to Marie.

"Hello, are you on the phone?" Her voice sounded shaky.

"I was but I can call them back when we finish. Nothing pressing. What's going on with you? I thought you would be at work. Is everything okay?"

"Yeah, everything is good. I just got this urge,

this unction while I was sitting at my desk. And I knew I needed to come home and call you . . ." She let the statement hang in midair, hoping that ManMan would pick it up and finish it for her.

"An urge for what? What kind of unction?" He didn't know what else to say, so he felt for the right thing and hoped for the best.

"An urge to make the call. To call Jerome back. Can we do that now, right now, before I lose the urge and the unction goes away?"

"Yeah, we can do that now. I'll be right there."

"Okay, I'll see you in a minute."

As he hung up the telephone, ManMan wondered what had changed Marie's mind. Why did she want to call now? Each time he had mentioned it in the previous days and then weeks, she had come up with some reason not to call. At first she told him she wanted to wait until she could take some time off from work. Then she said she didn't need to take time off and that she would be ready to make the call the next weekend. When the weekend came, she wouldn't answer the phone when he called. He knew she was avoiding him, so he didn't bother her, instead waiting for her to call him again. She did on Monday morning before she went to work. "I've been resting all weekend, Rayford. I'll call you when I get off work, okay?" He said okay and thought about it when he hung up the phone. She was still the scared little girl who didn't like to go in the dark because "*she couldn't tell what was in there. It might be something bad, real bad,*" she used to say. This darkness was scaring her, too. ManMan wasn't sure the fear was unjustified this time.

"Hey, come on in and sit down. Can I get you anything, Rayford?"

"No, I'm good."

"Well, let's do this before I start making excuses again. Do you still have the number?"

"Yeah, I have it right here." Marie passed him the phone, moving on the understanding that he would make the call. She still didn't know whether or not she would talk to Jerome this time. She doubted it though.

"Hello, yes, I'm trying to reach Jerome Grayson. He's in the infirmary and Dr. Bishop told me to ask for him when I called back." The same voice that had answered three weeks ago responded in the same monotone. "Yes, will you hold please?" Before ManMan could respond, there was silence and he knew she had put him on hold. He asked Marie if she wanted to go ahead and pick up the other phone. She shook her head no and sat there in the recliner opposite him. Her eyes were wide with expectation or anxiety – or fear. She hardly blinked at all, but she wasn't crying this time, either. She just sat there waiting for someone to come back on the line. Waiting to find out where her child was.

"Yes, this is Dr. Bishop. How may I help you?"

"Dr. Bishop, I'm calling again for Jerome Grayson. We spoke a few weeks ago and you told me to call back during this time. Is Jerome able to talk? Can I speak with him now?"

"Well, I'm just getting here, but let me see if he's awake. He's been waiting on your call, and I promised him he could speak to you whenever you did call again."

ManMan heard Dr. Bishop talking to Jerome through the muffle of the covered mouthpiece. He was trying to make sure Jerome was coherent enough to talk on the phone. After about a minute, Dr. Bishop uncovered the mouthpiece and spoke again. "Sir, are you Mr. Johnson, Rayford Johnson?"

"Yes, I am."

"Yes, it's Mr. Johnson," Dr. Bishop was speaking to Jerome. The prisoner must have given his consent for the conversation because the next voice ManMan heard was Jerome's.

"Hey, Man. I thought you wasn't going to call me back. I had figured you thought I was a fool or trying to trick you or something. Anyway, I'm glad you called back. I need to get all of this stuff off of me before . . . Well, anyway, I'm glad you called back."

There was silence and then ManMan thought he should clear his throat or make some kind of noise to let Jerome know he was there. He did and then began what was to become the first in a series of confession/questions & answer/unburden-my-soul-so-I-can-rest-in-peace conversations between him and the man who had taken away the woman he loved two decades ago.

"Yeah, I had to talk to Marie before I called you back. I didn't want to get into her business without asking her about it first."

"That makes good sense. She deserves at least that. Much more than that . . . That's why I wanted to talk to you and to her. So she'll know where Kal'eal is, or where he was the last time I heard anything . . ."

"That's what she wants to know basically. She said that anything you can tell her about that, she would really appreciate it."

There was another silence, like Jerome had changed his mind or had put the phone down.

"Hello," ManMan said after a few minutes of silence.

"Yeah, I'm here. I was just laying here thinking 'bout how bad I did Marie. How I messed her whole life up. From the time I came to Mississippi to the time she went back to Mississippi, I didn't do nothing but f . . . I'm sorry, Preacher. I didn't do nothing but mess up her life. And then to mess my son up, too. If I can still call him that, my son."

"I guess you can still call him that. He might not agree and Marie might not, either, but I guess he is still and will always be your son, your flesh and blood." ManMan wasn't really trying to be understanding and helpful, he simply wanted Jerome to go ahead and tell him where the child was. That's all he wanted so he wouldn't have to call him anymore and so that Marie could finally know, too.

"You probably wouldn't say that if you knew how bad I did Marie, and all the hell I put her through in Chicago. Have you ever sat down and talked to her about it? I guess she told her Mama, but knowing Marie, she didn't really tell nobody else the whole story. Except maybe you."

"Why do you think she would tell me, Jerome?"

"I ain't crazy, Preacher, and I wasn't crazy when we was kids either. I know you and Marie was made for each other. I knew that when I first came that summer. That's why I tried so hard to get her attention, to get her away from you, and from Mississippi. I knew if we had stayed, pregnant or not, she would have eventually gone back to you. To tell you the truth, I don't think she ever really left you. Her body just went with me to Chicago."

"Is that right? What makes you say that?"

"You can tell when a person really love you, even I know that. As much hell as I have raised in my life, I know my Mama loves me to this day. She is the only one who was in court every time I was before the judge. Even when she got sick one time and couldn't hardly walk, she made my sister bring her down to the courthouse. My sister be giving me them mean looks, cussing me with her eyes, but Mama always smiled at me and held her arms out to me. Then she'd start crying so loud, Man. Most of the time even the judge would feel sorry for her. Not enough to let me go, though. He would tell the officer to take my handcuffs off and let me hug my Mama before I go."

"How many times have you been in jail?" ManMan kept his questions short and to the point. He had a lot more of them to ask, but he was determined not to become truly concerned about Jerome. He just needed to get some information.

"Let me see. Five, six, seven, eight. This is my last time. This is the ninth time I been in prison. The judge told me this time I shouldn't even think about getting out. I would rot in here . . . I wonder if he knew what he was saying was true. 'Cause that's just what I'm doing – rotting away."

Marie sat there in the recliner opposite ManMan, pleading with her eyes. *Please hurry up and get him to tell you where Kal'eal is. Please hurry.* But there was nothing he could do short of just saying to Jerome, "Man, I'm really not interested in you. Can you please tell me where the child is? That's all I need to know." And even as empty as his heart was of any kind feelings toward Jerome, the Man of God couldn't be that cold. So he shrugged his shoulders as he looked toward Marie, letting her know he wasn't really getting the information they wanted.

"What do you mean when you say rotting away?" This seemed to shake Marie. She sort of frowned her face in a "*What did you say*" expression? She stood up and moved closer to ManMan, who pointed down the hall. Then he held his other hand up to his ear indicating she should go pick up the other phone. Marie understood and quickly went down the hall. When he figured she had made it, ManMan coughed to cover the sound of her taking the phone off the cradle. He could tell the line was open at the other end of the house. He asked his question again because Jerome had not yet answered.

"Did you hear my question, Jerome? What do you mean when you say rotting away?"

"Yeah, I heard you. I was just trying to figure out how to explain it. I'm sick, Man. Real sick. It's bad like they said it would be . . ."

"What's wrong with you? What's as bad as they said it would be?"

"You know what I got. You can put two and two together. The drugs and everything else I got into because of them . . . I got the HIV, Man. I'm HIV positive. The doctor say he think I might actually have full blown AIDS. He's waiting on some tests to come back. But I don't need no tests. I already know what they go' say. I already know."

They were both silent for a long time. ManMan didn't know what to say and Jerome wasn't able to say anything. He knew he was very sick, but the reality of the illness and its most likely outcome was sinking into him all over again. His silence said more than any words could. Marie felt the urge to cry or laugh or do something, but she remembered Jerome didn't know she was on the phone. Her emotions were going haywire and she wasn't sure she could control them. She thought she should quietly hang the phone up and just sit there on the side of her bed until Rayford was finished. But she knew she had to keep listening. She didn't want to miss a word Jerome said about her child.

"Anyway. Did you say you talked to Marie?"

"Yes, I did have a chance to talk with her. I told her you called and said you needed to get a message to her, to tell her where your son is."

"And what did she say when you told her that?"

"Well, she said she wants to know where he is if you know."

Another stretch of silence reminded the Man of God of what Marie had asked him earlier: "You don't think he's going to just come out and tell me where Kal'eal is, do you?" Despite their years of absence from one another and the little less than two years they were married, Marie must have really known Jerome like she thought she did. He was not going to make this quick or easy.

"When I got put in here this time, I had some people checking on some things for me, and one of them was finding my son. The other one was getting me out of here. 'Cause believe it or not, I'm actually innocent this time. I know everybody says it, but I really was in the wrong place at the wrong time, and just got caught up in a mess. When the judge looked at my record, he didn't even want to hear nothing from me. I tried to get the public defender to say something, she just told me to be quiet and pray for a miracle. So I wound up in here again, and for the last time probably. But I'm really innocent this time. You don't know any good lawyers, do you? I don't have much time left in this world but it sure would be good not to spend it in here. At least I could see my sisters again and meet some of my nieces and nephews."

As ManMan listened to Jerome, Marie's mind started to put it all together. Jerome had called Rayford's office pretending to want to talk to her, to tell her where their son was. But what he really wanted was to find a new lawyer. He figured that with all of his connections and business associations, Rayford could get him in touch with a good lawyer. This was just like him. He never gave anything without thinking he could get something in return. She was sick to her stomach when she thought about it. And if she didn't know before, she knew at that moment she still hated Jerome.

CHAPTER 15

SEVERAL DAYS HAD PASSED, TOO, since Mr. Johnson had told Dr. Barrette he wouldn't be taking the chemotherapy. Every two or three days the doctor called to talk first to Mr. Johnson, and then to Mrs. Johnson. He was trying to get someone to see the logic of his insistence on the treatments. He didn't want to lose Mr. Johnson as a patient or as a friend, and his experience told him that the chemotherapy could really help. It might even send the cancer into remission. But he had to convince someone in the Johnson household to believe him. So when he couldn't get through to Mr. Johnson or his wife, he thought about their children. He had gone to school with both of them. He and Rayford, Jr. (he thought that was his name) were only one year apart. The doctor had graduated before the architect, but they were close enough grade-wise to know each other. Dr. Barrette vaguely remembered a daughter, a little sister, too. Maybe he could find her.

The first thing he had to do was find out where the siblings were. "Sanquita, can you come here for a minute?" Sanquita Howard had been Dr. Barrette's nurse since he came back home and set up his own practice. She knew everything about the office, the patients, and the town in which they lived. She'd recently gotten married and returned from her honeymoon. Her new husband was still calling her at least every two or three hours, and they seemed to Dr. Barrette to be exceptionally happy.

"Yes, Sir, I'll be there in just a minute." She had to finish the notes on the information chart she was updating. She tried to do this right after the patient left the office. Otherwise, it could be very hard to keep up and she almost always forgot something Dr. Barrette told her to note. She always kept a small notepad with her, too. She would scribble notes in her own version of shorthand and then transfer them into the patient's folder. This was one of the things that made her an invaluable asset to the doctor she worked for, and Dr. Barrette couldn't imagine his office without her.

"Whenever you get a minute. I just need to ask you something."

"I'm coming. Just a minute," Nurse Howard said as she was closing her notes. By this time, though, she was already standing up and poised to go down the corridor to Dr. Barrette's private office. She grabbed her little notepad and was there in less than a minute.

"Yes, Sir, what do you need?"

"Just some information. Do you know Mr. Johnson's children? I think he has a son and a daughter, doesn't he?"

"Yes, Sir, I believe he does. You're talking about Mr. Rayford Johnson, right?"

"Yes. I'm trying to get in touch with the children . . ."

"Is his case that serious already?"

"No, no. He's still got plenty of time, but I want to make sure he has as much time as possible. He says he won't undergo the chemo. Says he doesn't want to get sicker and weaker than he has to. I don't know what I can say to make him change his mind. I've talked to him and to his wife. All she says is that it's not her body, so she can't help but to stand by her husband's decision. I'm really worried about him. I think that if I can talk to his children and get them to talk to him, maybe they can convince him to take the treatments. I've looked at the test results, and I really think the chemo could help send the cancer into remission."

"Do you know whether or not he's told them about the cancer? That could be an issue, you know.

If he hasn't told them already. And then there's the whole privacy issue, too."

"I know. That's something I've thought about, too. But I would risk it if I could just get them to talk to him about taking the treatments. I'll try not to go in detail, but if it takes that . . . I really think it could save him, Sanquita, I really do."

"Well, I know his daughter still lives here in Waynesboro with her parents. She was in a nursing class with me, but I don't think she finished the program. She started doing some singing and acting. As a matter of fact, she was in that show that was here a few weeks ago. Now the son, Rayford, Jr., I think they call him ManMan, he lives out of state. Maybe in Georgia? I'd have to make a call or two to find out for sure."

"Can you do that for me? I'd like to talk to him first. I'll try to think up some reason to say I called him and try to feel him out, to see if he knows anything. I won't tell him if he doesn't. That wouldn't be right or fair to his father. But I pray he already knows something. So, yeah, go ahead and find out where he lives. See if you can get a number, too."

"Okay, give me a few minutes. I'll work on it until I find out something. Is that all you need?"

"Yes, if you can take care of that, it would help me a lot. I might even let you go home early today.

To check on your new *husband*." He said this with a sly grin. The change in his nurse was noticeable, and it was good. So he supported her in marriage and the happiness it brought her.

"Alright now, I'm go' hold you to that!" She laughed as she went back to her office, thinking about just who she could call to find out what she needed to know. Sandra might know. LaShawn might know, too. But she was almost positive Marie would know. And that's who she called.

The call waiting beep on the phone shocked ManMan. He didn't know whether or not to answer it, and Marie was down the hall so he couldn't ask her. Thinking quickly, he broke the silence that had fallen between he and Jerome again. "Jerome, can you hold on a minute. I have another call."

"I guess I can, Man, it ain't like I have any pressing engagements to get to. Go ahead, I'll be here." Jerome answered with a bit of humor, and ManMan had to admit, it was a good comeback. He clicked over, but didn't answer. Marie took her cue.

"Hello," she said from the bedroom extension.

"Hey, Girl, are you on the phone? This is Quita Howard."

"As a matter of fact I am. Can I call you back? Are you at Dr. Barrette's office?"

"Yeah, I'm still at work, but I'm working on getting off early."

"Okay, I'll call you back in a little bit. Is anything to matter?"

"Naw, I just need to ask you something. It's about Rayford, Jr."

ManMan was surprised to hear his name. He hoped that Marie would ask what she wanted to know about him, but again, he couldn't see her so he had no way of letting her know to ask. Marie must have been as curious as he was.

"What about him?" She didn't want to seem too anxious, nor did she want to have to wonder what Sanquita wanted to know about Rayford. If she wasn't mistaken, there was the slightest twinge of "What you asking about the man I love for?" in her voice. She laughed at her own self when she thought about it later.

"I was wondering if you know how to get in touch with him. It's for Dr. Barrette."

Marie didn't know how to respond at first, then she thought of what to tell Sanquita without lying and without saying 'Yeah, he's on the phone with us now.'

"Well, I think he came home for the funeral. Shawn called me and told me she saw his car at the house."

"What funeral? Somebody in their family died?

I hadn't even heard. But Girl, you're on the phone. I'll call you back or you can call me back. I'm about to get off in the next hour or so. I'll call you back, okay?"

"Okay, call me when you get off, if Derrick let you. I know how *busy* he keeps you."

"You know it, Hon, and I am truly blessed! I'll talk to you later."

"Okay, bye."

Sanquita was glad that she had accomplished her task so quickly, but she wondered who had died, too. She'd find that out later, but right now she was going to tell Dr. Barrette what Marie had said.

"Doc, I have some good news for you. My sources tell me that Rayford Jr. is actually in Waynesboro now. He came home for a funeral and is probably still here. I imagine he's staying at his parents' house, so do you want me to get their number before I leave?"

"What do you mean before you leave? It's only three o'clock. We don't leave until five, do we?"

"Naw, now Dr. B. You said that if I found out what you needed to know, I could go home. I know you haven't forgotten that quick. Now I'm going on in here and find this number for you, and then I'm going home, right?"

"I guess so, Miss Pickens, I mean Mrs. Howard. You can go on home. I'll be okay here all by myself."

"Good. I'm glad to hear it."

The relationship between the doctor and his head nurse had always been easy. From the first day she came to interview for the position, Sanquita had been the sunshine of the office and could lift Dr. Barrette's spirit on the worst of days. She had seen him weep over the loss of patients and cry at the birth of children. She had been with him when his own father died and understood why Mr. Johnson's case was so personal to him. He had become a sort of surrogate father for Dr. Barrette, and the doctor wanted to do all he could to keep this father in his life. To tell the truth, her boss was scared and Sanquita knew it. She would do all she could to help, the least of which was finding out where Rayford, Jr. was and making sure Dr. Barrette knew, too.

She pulled Mr. Johnson's file and walked back to Dr. Barrette's office. To her surprise, he had already clicked open his laptop's contact database and was staring at the number on the screen. When she got to the door, Sanquita was going to make a joke about him always asking her to do stuff he already had done or had the capacity to do as easily as she could. But something told her that this was not a joking time. She stood there a minute and then ventured into the office. She sensed that her boss needed more than an employee. He needed a friend.

"Doc, I know it's not my business and you didn't ask me, but do you want some advice?"

"Please. I could use some right now."

"Well the first thing you need to do, as you already know, is pray. I know you want to do what you think is best, what your medical training and experience tell you is best, but God always knows more than we ever will. And the other thing you have to really think about is how Mr. Johnson feels."

"That's the hardest part. He said he won't budge and that he doesn't want to get sicker than he has to be. He's right. I can't guarantee that he won't feel worse than he's ever felt in his life if he begins that chemo. I can't guarantee that it will do any good. But I can almost guarantee that he will certainly die without it . . ."

"Now wait, Doc. That's where we've got to part company. There is no guarantee that he will die. Didn't you hear what I just said? God knows more than we will ever know and He can do more than any medical procedure can do." Sanquita didn't want to offend Dr. Barrette, but she forgot herself when it came to issues of faith verses medicine. She loved her job and was fascinated by the medical works she'd witnessed in her years of nursing. But when push came to shove, she would always put faith and God's Divine provision and, in some cases, intervention, over medical knowledge and ability.

"I know," Dr. Barrette resigned. "But I just want to make sure I've explored every option and done everything that can be done."

"You can't explore options with someone's life who has already chosen the option they think is best for them. It sounds like Mr. Johnson has already chosen."

They were quiet for a moment, and then Dr. Barrette smiled and chuckled quietly. "I know you're ready to go," he said, trying to lighten the mood. "You can go on home. I'll stick by my promise."

"Well, I guess I can stay a little while longer. It's good to make him wait . . ."

They both laughed and then sat in silence.

CHAPTER 16

THE SECOND CONVERSATION BETWEEN JEROME and ManMan, with Marie listening, had ended shortly after the interruption from Sanquita. Jerome asked about a lawyer and waited for ManMan's response.

"Well, I don't know about that, Jerome. Of course I know lawyers, but I didn't really call to help you find a lawyer. I called to see what message you wanted me to give Marie, to find out where her son is. That's what I called for." He sounded short and didn't really care. ManMan was getting the same feeling Marie had all along: Jerome wanted something. He didn't want to lead Jerome to believe he was even close to getting anything from him, certainly not the possibility of getting out of jail. Just because he might not be guilty this time, he was still guilty of hurting Marie and causing her to lose her son. He'd taken her away from Mississippi, from safety and security, from her mother, from her support base, and then abandoned her in every way.

No, ManMan decided at that moment, he wouldn't have anything to do with Jerome being free. He simply would not do it.

Jerome came back with a short retort and gave ManMan an ultimatum. He might well have known Marie was on the line, too, because his statement was really to her and not to ManMan.

"I'll tell you what," Jerome said with sudden arrogant confidence, "You talk with Marie and see what she says. Maybe she knows a good lawyer. Maybe she'll be willing to help me get out of here, seeing as how I'm the only one who really knows where the boy is. My son, I mean. Our son. You don't have to help me. But I just believe Marie will be willing to help me when she knows what I have to offer. You get what I'm saying?"

"I get what you're saying, Jerome. I hear what you're not saying, too. You're saying that you're the same person you were when we were young. The same person Marie told me you were . . ."

"Oh, so you have talked to her about me. I should have known it. For all I know she might be right there with you. Ya'll might be living together or something, for all I know."

"If that were the case, what business would it be of yours? I know you don't feel like you have any ties to Marie. . ."

"See, that's where *you* are mistaken, Preacher. I

do still have ties to her. She is still my wife! There ain't no divorce papers."

ManMan was stunned into silence. He almost lost his breath. Even if Jerome was lying, it was still hard to entertain the possibility that he and Marie might still be married.

Jerome invaded ManMan's momentary confusion in a voice that was gaining more and more confidence the longer the conversation went on. "Oh, you didn't know that, did you? Miss Marie, or shall I say, Mrs. Grayson didn't tell you that part did she? While she was probably pouring her heart out to you and getting you to feel all sorry for her, she didn't tell you she was still my wife. Well, I'm telling you that she is!"

ManMan wanted to slam the phone down in Jerome's ear and go immediately down the hall to ask Marie if what he had just heard was true. Before he could do either, he saw Marie in his periphery. She was standing on the other side of the room. Her face didn't look particularly distressed, just like she felt a bit guilty. Her eyes seemed to say, "*Here's another disappointment for you, Rayford. Let's see how you deal with this.*"

"Even if you are still legally married, you can be sure that Marie has no desire to be a wife to you, not after the way you treated her. A divorce is the least of the concerns she will have to deal with. You know those lawyers I told you I knew? They will have divorce papers drawn up and processed before you can even say the word appeal." ManMan was getting angrier, and it was showing.

"Listen, Man of God, don't get upset with me. You need to talk to Marie so she can tell you I'm telling the truth. She can also tell you what she wants to do about getting me a new lawyer so I can get out of here. Don't worry, I don't want Marie as a wife anymore. There's not enough of me left to want that." After a moment of silence, he said, almost as an afterthought, "And I will sign the divorce papers. But you go' have to help me, too. I hate to be such a bastard, but I've got to think about me, too."

"From what I hear, that's never been a problem for you."

"Look, like I said, Man of God. You and Marie talk about things and do what you think is best. I've got information about the boy and I can give it to her. I've got to have some help, though. Something in return. Just give me a call back when you talk with her. We'll go from there."

He handed the phone to someone and the dial tone soon followed. ManMan held the phone to his ear, trying to quickly figure out what he would say to Marie. He wished she was still down the hall. He needed time to think about this "still married" thing. He was in shock. He needed time. When he finally hung up the phone, he asked a question, waited for the answer, and then made a statement.

"Is what Jerome said true? Are you still married?"

"Yes."

"Okay, I need just a little bit of time. I have to think about this. I'll have to call you later. Maybe tomorrow. But I will call you."

Marie's head was spinning for a long time after Rayford left her house. She didn't know exactly *why* she hadn't told him she and Jerome were still legally married. It wasn't a deliberate deception, but she had a feeling that Rayford had taken it as such. When she came home to Mississippi, she didn't have any money. She went back to school, got her GED, and then a degree. It was really the last thing on her mind. There were no men she had actually ever considered marrying, that is, until Rayford came back into the picture.

God, this is the last thing I need right now. You know I wasn't trying to hide anything from him. I hadn't even thought about it. Well, yes I had, but I was going to tell him. Help me, Holy Ghost. For real, I need Your help. Jerome is already going to give me a hard time about all of this. I don't need Rayford questioning my motives. Lord, have mercy. Just show him my heart, Father. I can't do anything else or say anything else that will convince him I'm for real. Show him my heart, so he'll know. And

God, I need You to work on Jerome, too. He's the only one who might know where my child is. I need You to move by Your Spirit and change his heart. However You need to do it, I need You to make him tell me what he knows.

When he got home that afternoon, ManMan was greeted by his mother's request for a moment of his time. She sensed that something was on his mind but still needed to give him the message from Dr. Barrette.

"He called this afternoon and asked that you give him a call or come by the office," she said with resignation.

"Do you know what he wants, Mama?"

"Not really, but it's probably something to do with your Daddy. We just went to see him the other day. He tried to talk to your Daddy about the chemotherapy again."

"And what did Daddy say about it?" His questions were short and to the point. He hoped she wouldn't take it personally, but Marie, Jerome and "still married" weighed heavily on his mind.

"Well, he said what he said in the beginning: he's not going to do it. He said he didn't want to be sicker than he had to be trying to get well. The Lord will do what He thinks is best. That's what he told Dr. Barrette. He has his mind made up." She let her voice trail off and stared out of the window.

Her husband was outside in her flower garden and she could see him from the window. It was seldom he went in the garden, always calling it "my wife's garden" and declaring, "I ain't fixin' to go in there and mess nothin' up!" But that afternoon, he was in the garden gathering flowers.

"I'll call him. But not right now. Do you think it's urgent?"

"He didn't say," she said. But her eyes and her mind were still on her husband. "But if you don't feel like calling him right now, it can wait. Your Daddy is doing alright. Look at him out there picking flowers . . ."

He joined her at the window, and they watched husband and father, neither saying anything, both being moved beyond words at the image. Mr. Johnson was kneeling in the garden, pulling a few vagabond weeds from among the legitimate buds and flowers. His mouth was moving, but they couldn't tell whether he was singing or talking or what . . .

. . . *Father, I'm blessed. This sickness trying to rattle me, but I still know I'm blessed. I got my wife, my children. Even a doctor that care about me. God, I'm blessed and I'm grateful. I don't know how long I'll be here, be able to come out here and pull grass from among these flowers, but I can do it now. I'm glad about it. My hands still strong, my mind still good, my legs still work,* and I still got breath in my body. I'm just glad, Father. You the only one who knows what's go' happen or come of all this. You the only one who know whether this go' take me out of here or whether You go' heal me. I just want to let You know how I feel about it. I want to live a lot a more years. I want to see my children get old and gray like me. I want to be here with my wife until it's time for her to come Home to be with You. That's what I want. But Lord, I know You got a plan and a time for everything in this world, and that means for my life, too. I know that. You done blessed me to set aside some money and this land so they won't have to worry about nothing, and I thank You for that. God, I guess what I'm saying is that I want You to do what You know is best, but I don't want them to hurt when I leave here. They'll have everything they need, but I know they hearts will be broke when I leave here. And mine is breaking just to think about leaving them. The only thing that make me even want to consider taking that chemo is the fact that I might be helping them feel more safe. It might make them feel better that I'm doing something to try to get well. But Lord, I just don't want to go through all of that. Help 'em understand that part of it. I just don't want to be gettin' sicker and sicker trying to get better. Them having to watch me be sick and heaving and all of that. God, I don't want to put them through all of that. I would rather just spend the time that I do have with them, just being me. Yeah, that's what I want. So if You don't see fit to heal me, it's alright. I've *lived a good, full life and You don't owe me nothin'. I'm mighty partial to You, Sir. Mighty partial . . ."*

When he started laughing and got up off his knees to come in the house, ManMan tried to get away from the window before his father made it in the house. He just kept going down the hall to his room. But Mrs. Johnson didn't try to hide the fact that she had been watching him. Mr. Johnson came in the house with a beautiful bunch of flowers, roses, forget-me-nots, tulips, and daisies. He gave them to her and kissed her lightly on the cheek, "They not as pretty as you, but it's the best I could do on short notice." She smiled gently and took the flowers out of his hands. While the water was running in the vase, she felt water on her own face. For the first time since he told her about the cancer, she was crying at the thought of him possibly not being there one day to say things like that, to give her flowers from her own garden. Her heart got heavy all of a sudden, but she tried to be strong. She didn't want him worrying. So she began to do what she thought would signal to her husband that she was okay. *"I sing because I'm happy. I sing because I'm free. His eye is on the sparrow, and I know He watches me."*

Rayford, Sr. looked back over his shoulder as he passed by his wife. She turned her face from him, so he knew from years of experience that she was crying. He went and took the flowers from her and finished filling up the vase. He arranged the flowers as she continued to hum and wipe her eyes. Without a word, he took her hand and, with the vase in his free hand, led her to the table. He set the vase down and pulled out a chair for her, still without a word. He pulled out his handkerchief from his pocket and thoughtfully wiper her eyes, and she smiled as she held his hand close to her face. His eyes were beginning to water, too, but he still began:

"You know, I was out there in the garden talking to the Lord. And it's go' be alright. I know it just sound like something to say, but it really will, Baby. . . . You see these flowers here? It's all kind of 'em in this vase and in the garden, too. When you think about it, Honey, that's what the past 33 years been like for us. We've had some real good times, like this rose here. But it's been some rough times, too, like these thorns. But when you sit down and look at all of the colors, the flowers, together, it's still a pretty picture. This thing is just one of the thorns, Sweetheart. God made the flowers and the thorns, and they all work to give Him the Glory. I don't know what He go' decide to do about this. I don't know. And I go from being scared to being mad to being just down right confused. But right now, I'm just still. You know what I mean? I'm just still about it. The cancer. The therapy. All of it. I'm just at peace, and I want you to be, too. If I leave here today or tomorrow, I will wake up in Glory. And you know the first thing I'm go' tell God? Thank You for the years You gave me. Thank You for my sweet, sweet, beautiful wife. She made my time on earth better than any other man I know. She gave me comfort when I couldn't be comforted. She gave me rest when my soul was weary. She rubbed my head when it was hurting. She gave me some good children. That's what I'm go' tell Him, Honey. I won't ask Him why or how or why not or when. I'm just go' tell Him Thank You – for giving me you."

Mr. Johnson stopped talking but never let his eyes leave Mrs. Johnson. He kissed her hand and held it close to his heart. She couldn't explain or understand it, but her fears were immediately stilled. All she could feel was the love he felt for her, and that gave her immense comfort and peace.

CHAPTER 17

It had been three weeks since Marie had talked to ManMan. She hadn't seen his car in front of his parents' house, on her way to and from work on the route that took her at least ten minutes out of the way. She didn't know what to do but was sure the love of her life was gone for good this time. The first time it was her fault, she had walked away following Jerome. This time was her fault, too, because she hadn't done anything to officially detach herself from him. Her heart didn't know what to feel, but it felt a lot like it was breaking.

ManMan didn't know what to do when he left Marie's that day. He was tired and confused and mad. Mad at who? At Marie? At God? Although he could have made good arguments for both, the truth was, he was mad at himself. He tried to convince himself that it was Marie and Jerome, but he knew better. It was all on him. Regardless of what he knew or didn't know about the marriage, about

Jerome being in jail, about whatever, he was still responsible because of what God told him to do. He knew God had sent him back into Marie's life "for such a time as this," yet he had walked away. He announced to his mother and father that he had to go back to Atlanta, something had happened at work and he needed to be there. He had not even returned Dr. Barrette's call about his father. It was all just too much for him. How could God send all of this into his life now? Things were going so well for him.

He kept thinking like that for about seven days, and then God got tired of it. ManMan couldn't sleep, and when he did, Marie and Jerome and his father were always in his dreams/nightmares. Really in his dream/nightmare because it was the same one over and over again. It always began with his father sitting on what looked like a throne or a judgment seat. He was leaning back in the chair, his head resting, and his eyes closed. There were two tables, Marie and Jerome were sitting at one, ManMan was sitting at the other. The tables were facing each other in the middle of the room. Somewhere behind him, he could never see her, was his mother. She was crying through the whole dream, quietly sobbing like she had that day looking out the window at her husband. Jeannine was there, or her voice was, singing "This Too Will Pass."

In the dream, Mr. Johnson was asking ManMan questions, but never looked at him while he tried to answer. He didn't really seem interested in what ManMan had to say or he already knew the answers. *"What did you come home for?" "When did you decide to leave?" "Did God tell you to come home?" "Did God tell you to leave?" "Do you know who your Father is?" "Do you know who your father is?" "Do you know Marie Carter?" "Do you know Marie Carter?" "Do you know Marie Carter?"* Each time, the questions were the same. And not one time did his father give ManMan a chance to answer any of them. After he was finished with the barrage of accusatory questions, instead of looking at ManMan, the Mr. Johnson in the dream would look at Jerome and Marie, as if he expected or wanted them to answer the questions. They didn't say anything or even look at Mr. Johnson. They looked at ManMan.

His own voice would always wake him up. He was trying to answer the questions in the dream, to explain himself, and started answering them aloud in his sleep. When he woke up fully, his pillow was wet. He didn't know if it was from sweat or tears. After the third night of no sleep and the same dream, he knew he had to do something. God was not going to just let this go or let him get back to business as usual. It wouldn't be that simple. He had to do something.

God, I know I messed up. I shouldn't have left like I did or when I did. I know I was wrong. Forgive me. Tell me what I need to do now. Should I go back home? Should I call Marie? I don't know, God. I'm scared. To tell the truth about it, I'm just scared. I don't know if I can handle all of this. Daddy. Marie. Jerome. The child. It's just so much, God. I don't know if I can do it . . . But I'll try. Help me, Holy Ghost. I need You now. I need Your strength and Your Power to do this. I can't go back on my own. I need You to make the way plain and straight. I need You to guide me.

Before he could finish his prayer, the phone rang. It was his office manager, Tracy Scott, calling him. ManMan had only been in and out in the last three weeks. His body was back in Atlanta, but of course his mind and his spirit were in Mississippi.

"Hello."

"Good morning, Mr. Johnson, this is Tracy."

"Yes, is everything alright?" ManMan realized he was being short, but he really didn't have the presence of mind to be kind and polite and patient. His spirit was so heavy. It was all he could do to carry on conversation and just be around people who were not his family, particularly his father, and Marie.

"Yes, Sir, everything is fine here at the office. But you just got an emergency call."

"From who? Is it my Daddy? Is it from home?"

"No, Sir. It's from the same Jerome Grayson who called when you were in Mississippi. He wouldn't tell me what he wanted. He's still on the other line and insisted that he talk to you right now. He said it was a matter of life and death, otherwise I would not have disturbed you at home, Sir. Do you want to speak with him? If not, I can handle him."

For a few seconds, ManMan couldn't think or breathe. His mind went totally blank. When he did come back to reality, he still couldn't say anything.

"Mr. Johnson, are you still there? I can get him off the phone if I need to. Then I'll call you back and let you know what he wanted. Or you can hold on . . ."

ManMan almost let Tracy put him on hold but something shot through his body. It reminded him of that first Sunday after Travis had almost died. There had been many other encounters with the Holy Spirit, but none like that first time. And now he knew the Holy Spirit was moving on him. He had to take the call. He had to talk to Jerome. He didn't have any choice in the matter. He had asked God to help him, to speak to him, and He had done just that.

"No, Mr. Scott, you can put him through. I'll talk to him."

"Yes, Sir."

ManMan waited for the phone to click back

over. He tried to let his mind rest and not think about what Jerome could have possibly wanted. It probably wasn't really a life or death situation, he was sure of that. Jerome was probably just trying to get him back on the phone to talk about the lawyer again. Or to find out what Marie had said in response to his demands. ManMan knew it would take patience to deal with this. He tried to sneak in a prayer, but before he could get out a "Help me, Holy Ghost," he heard the phone click.

"Hello." When no voice spoke from the other end, ManMan ventured to say something himself.

"Hey, Man. What's up? I ain't heard from you in a while. I just thought I better call you back before . . ." Jerome's voice trailed off and it sounded like he was actually choked up, fighting back tears.

"Before what? Before you decided you weren't going to tell Marie what you know about your son unless I get you a new lawyer? Or before you figured out another way to mess with her mind? Before what, Jerome?" He didn't realize it before he took the call, but he was mad. The anger he had at the end of their last conversation had not gone anywhere. It was still right there simmering in his spirit. Before he knew it, The Man of God was talking almost at the top of his lungs to Jerome on the phone.

". . . Actually I meant before I die . . ."

It took a few minutes for ManMan to comprehend what Jerome had said. *He said "Before I die." Before he dies. What is he up to now?*

"The doctor said it could be any day now, and I'm scared. I don't know what to do. I don't know what to expect. I wish I had listened all those days in church, cause right now, I need something to hold on to. . . Are you still there, Rayford?"

"Yeah, I'm here." What else could he say? His anger caused him speak with such wrath and judgment, and now he was trying to deal with the conviction of the Holy Spirit and with the idea of Jerome's death. The other crucial thing was that Jerome needed salvation. He hadn't known how to say it or perhaps didn't know what he needed, but his words sent a clear signal to the Man of God. Jerome was scared to die not just because it was the end of life, but more crucially because he didn't know where he would spend eternity.

"I know I been messing around and giving Marie hell, but I'm for real now. I ain't go' be here too much longer and I need to tell her what I know about Kal'eal. Where he is and all of that. Do you think she'll come up here to see me before I die?" Jerome was using the word "die" just like it was nothing. He had resigned himself to the appearance of things and what the doctor had told him. To ManMan, he sounded like he *was* for real this time.

He made no mention of lawyers or his innocence. His mission was single and clear: he needed to get things straight before he went to whatever afterlife was awaiting him.

As he stood outside the prison gates waiting to be let in by the guard, ManMan remembered the conversation but was having trouble remembering how he had wound up there, outside the prison gates to see Jerome – and without Marie. He did remember calling Mr. Scott back after he hung up with Jerome. He had told Mr. Scott to book him on the next flight to Chicago and to arrange for a rental car to be waiting on him when he got there. He remembered packing a few things. He remembered the trip to the airport. As always, there was roadwork going on and he was almost late for the flight. He remembered thinking about his father and Marie. He remembered calling Mr. Scott back and telling him not to tell them where he went, but to call him on his cell phone immediately if either of them called. It wasn't that he wanted to keep his trip from anyone, especially Marie, but he just felt the Unction and he knew he wasn't supposed to tell her yet. So there he stood, palms sweating, knees weak, heart racing, as the guard opened the gate and coldly said, "Alright, follow me."

He had only been inside a prison two other

times in his life, each time for business. His firm designed the upgrades for two other state facilities and each time ManMan had personally gone to supervise the renovations. It was not that he didn't trust anyone else with the jobs, but again, it was just Unction - he knew he had to be there himself. Maybe it was preparation for this moment, when he began a series of visits with the man he had told God he could die without ever seeing again.

CHAPTER 18

THE ONLY THING THAT KEPT Marie's mind together during those first three weeks was the hope that ManMan might just show up again like he had for the funeral. Just like then, she wanted to call his mother and ask if she knew where he was or when he was coming back. But, like then, she didn't call. She stopped by the house on her way home from work. When she rang the doorbell, she immediately wished she could take it back and retract the sound. Mrs. Johnson came to the door knowing already why Marie was there.

"Hey there, Sweetie. Come on in. I was wondering if you were going to come back to visit us since Rayford, Jr. was gone. It surely is good to see you. Come on around and have a seat. Can I get you something to drink? I just made some tea and you know we always have some coffee brewing."

"No, Ma'am, I'm fine. I really stopped by to see if you all have heard from Rayford since he left. I haven't talked to him since then." She ended the sentence there, hoping Mrs. Johnson would fill in the missing details.

"Well, we heard from him when he first got back to Atlanta but not since then. He's doing fine, though. Jeannine said she gets an email from him almost every day. He's doing fine, Baby . . . But that isn't all you want to know, is it?"

"No, Ma'am, it's not. I need to know if he said anything about me before he left. Anything about what we talked about . . ."

"No, he didn't. Is there something in particular he should have mentioned?"

"Well, I might as well tell you, Mrs. Johnson. Jerome called Rayford's office while he was here. He pretended he wanted to get a message to me about Kal'eal, our son, and Rayford called him back while he was at my house. First he told us that he was real sick. He didn't know I was on the phone, though. Then Jerome started sounding like himself and insisted that the only way he would tell me anything was if Rayford got him a new lawyer and helped him get out of prison. And then Jerome told him we were still married. After that, Rayford just left the house and I haven't seen or talked to him since." Marie let it all fall out of her mouth quickly before she lost the nerve to tell it. She didn't want to keep anything covered anymore. ManMan's reaction to hidden information, no matter how innocent the hiding was, taught her quickly that it's best to put everything out there. Regardless of how the other person took it, regardless of the consequences, it's always best to tell the truth to those you love. Marie wished she'd remembered that earlier.

Mrs. Johnson was quiet for a minute, replaying what she had just heard in her mind. The truth was, she had heard Marie and was not the least bit bothered about any of it. She had heard, seen, and lived through worse. What she was really trying to figure out was whether to call ManMan right then, with Marie there, or to wait until she left. She quickly decided that if she did either, it would be the latter, and turned to look at Marie before responding to what she had heard.

"May, you remember when you left here to go to Chicago? Do you remember what your Mama told you that day? She said, '*Don't get up there and feel like you got to stay. You'll always have a home here. If it ain't what you thought it would be, come home. If you can't come, I'll come get you. If I can't come, I'll send somebody for you. You can always come home.*' Do you remember that?"

"Yes, Ma'am, I do."

"And when you did come home, wasn't she true to her word? Didn't she take you in without asking any questions until you were ready to answer them?"

"Yes, Ma'am, she did."

"Now do you remember when your Mama left this world, and I was there with you by her bedside?"

"Yes, Ma'am," Marie said through the tears that were freely flowing down her face by now. She wasn't sure where Mrs. Johnson was going, but the questions were stirring up strong emotions in her.

"I told your Mama that night that come what may, I would do whatever I could to take care of you. I promised her that until me and my husband leave this world and come join her in Glory, you would always have somewhere to go and somebody to take care of you. Do you think your Mama believed me?"

"I know she believed you. She whispered in my ear, 'Alright, I can go now.' And that's when she closed her eyes."

"Now, May, I said all of that to say this: I'm a woman of my word. I tried to fulfill the promise I made to your Mama . . ."

"I know you have, Mrs. Johnson, and I'm grateful for all you did then and have done since then . . ."

"As long as I have strength in my body, I'm going to give you any kind of help you need. If you need somebody to talk to, some money, somewhere to stay, something to eat, whatever you need: all you have to do is ask. I Love You like my own. To me, you are my own. Do you believe that? Do you know that?"

"Yes, Ma'am, I know."

"But regardless of how much I Love You and how much I want to provide you with comfort, safety, and security, I can't be a mouthpiece for my child to you. I can't tell you how he felt about what he heard or how he's feeling now. I don't know any of that because he hasn't talked to me. And if he had talked to me and asked me not to repeat it, I still couldn't tell you. But this one thing I do know. I know my child well enough to know that he still loves you. He never really stopped loving you. Now I wouldn't dare try to tell you what to do, and I usually don't get into my children's personal lives, but this time, I'll make an exception. My advice to you, Marie, is to do whatever you have to to get word to Rayford, Jr. that you need him, if you do. Get word to him that you want to talk to him, if you do. Get word to him that you didn't mean to deceive him, if you didn't. Just tell him the truth, Child, and let him work through it however he needs to. If he doesn't respond like you thought he would or like you wanted him to, you have to be prepared for that, too. He might tell you he understands and that all is well. He might tell you he's had enough and that he's not going any further with any of it. Just be ready for which ever way it goes. If you really want to talk to him, you've got to do it. You know how, with all of that internet and stuff at your office. I think you came by here for me to tell you it's okay to call him. I can't do that. I don't have that right. You've got to make the decision, one way or the other, and deal with the consequences."

Mrs. Johnson reached over to the end table for a box of tissues and offered Marie some. She hadn't stopped crying since the mention of her mother's final words. She knew Mrs. Johnson was right and if she wanted to contact ManMan, she would have to do it. No one could give her permission to do that but God and herself. Marie was already pretty sure that God was saying yes. As Mrs. Johnson had said, Marie knew she really went to the house to get an "Okay, here's the number. Go on and call him." She should have known better.

But even if she had gotten the number from Mrs. Johnson at that moment, it would have done her no good. ManMan wasn't at home in Atlanta. He wasn't at the office, either. He was walking down the long, cold, stale-smelling corridor that led to the infirmary at Illinois State Prison. He had arrived in Chicago about two hours earlier and picked up the rental car Mr. Scott arranged for him. He grabbed a quick lunch and then drove to the prison. He sat in the car for a long time, he wasn't sure how long, but for some reason he was really nervous. It felt like he was going into the prison to serve a sentence for some crime he had committed. The only difference was that he was going in of his own free will.

Images of Marie and his father raced through his mind as he sat trying to get up the nerve to go to the gate. They were the two people who were almost always at the forefront when he got up in the morning and when he lay down at night. Not that his mother, Jeannine, and his company weren't important, but they had taken a backseat to Marie, the woman he loved, and his father, the man by whom he measured the success or failure of every event in his life. He decided while he was sitting there to call both of them immediately upon his exit from the prison. He needed to connect with them again, not for them, but for himself. He might tell Marie where he was, and he might not. He might tell his father that Dr. Barrette had wanted to talk to him before he left, and he might not. ManMan was feeling so confused and anxious until he knew the first thing he had to do before he talked to Jerome, Marie, or his father. He needed to pray.

The only thing I know for sure, God, is that I'm scared and confused. I don't know why You have brought me to this place, why You have led me back to Marie, why You have allowed this disease to show up in my father's body. God, I am afraid that I can't handle all of it. I want to believe it will all work out, that everything will come out well, but I've got to tell You the truth if I don't tell anybody else: I'm scared. Father, help my unbelief. Holy Spirit, I need You to strengthen my heart. I can't do this by myself. I can't be all of these things to all of these people without Your help. I know You will never leave me nor forsake me, but I just need to feel Your Presence right now, Father. Before I walk in here and talk to this man, I need You to show up, God. Pour Yourself into my spirit right now, God, and be the Words I'm supposed to say. Be my eyes, God, so I can see his soul. Be my ears so I can hear his heart. Take control, Holy Spirit, and hide me behind the Power of You . . .

The guard's knock on the window surprised him, and ManMan realized he had been sitting in the car a long time. He hit the power button and let the window down.

"Good afternoon, Officer. How are you?" The guard was not smiling, and ManMan didn't want to give him any reason to suspect that anything was out of order.

"I'm fine, Sir. May I ask the purpose of your visit? You've been sitting here for more than an hour. Are you here to see someone?" The guard's words were, in themselves, non-threatening, but his tone would have struck fear in the heart of the most hardened criminal. Strangely, though, ManMan was absolutely calm, calmer that he had been in several weeks.

He answered with absolute surety, "Yes, I am here to see someone. But I needed to get myself together first, so I was praying." He didn't know how the guard would react and didn't really care. The prayer, although interrupted, had done what it needed to do. His mind was calm, his heart was easy, and his spirit was strengthened.

It must have showed because the guard's demeanor changed, too. "Oh, well if that's what you're doing, take as long as you need." He turned toward a security tower and signal to the guard there that everything was okay. "Take your time, Man. I know what prayer can do, after thirteen years of doing this, believe you me, I know. Just give me a signal, blow your horn or something when you get ready to get out of the car. I'll come back to walk you up to the gate. It'll go a little easier if I go with you." He turned to walk away, but didn't get very far before ManMan stopped him.

"Well, I might as well go with you now, so you won't have to walk all the way back out here. I'm ready now."

"You sure?"

"Yes, I'm sure."

The guard, whom ManMan learned was Isaac Johnson, no relation, seemed anxious to talk to someone "from the outside." It felt to ManMan like the guard was as bound as the inmates. But as he listened, he knew that was not the case at all. While they walked across the huge visitor's parking lot, Isaac provided a brief but in-depth synopsis of his life. He had begun working at the prison when he was thirty, after having spent seven years in the military as a soldier. Although he had not seen any battle, his experience he said "was rich" and he "wouldn't take anything for it." The prison job was just supposed to be for a few months while he found something else. He had to provide for his family during the transition from the steadiness of a military income to whatever he was going to do after his honorable discharge. A prison job couldn't be that hard, and it certainly wouldn't be permanent.

But, contrary to what he thought it would be, "This has been the toughest and most challenging thing I've ever done," Isaac confided in The Man of God. "I mean when I first started coming to work, it was hard. Seeing men, most of them just like me, young and black, being shackled and chained, being hollered at and sometimes called everything but a Child of God was hard, Brother. I swore after the first day I wouldn't come back. But I kept coming because I had a wife and three children to provide for. And then one day, one of the men said something that made me realize that I couldn't just walk away, even if I did find another job. He said, 'Man, you walk around here like you done lost your best friend. If you come in here with your head down, a free man, what you expect the rest of us to do? How we 'sposed to have any hope? You got to cheer up now. We need you to bring us some hope from the outside.' I heard everything he said, and he was right. But you know what stuck with me? When he said 'We need you.' From that day on, I tried to come here with that in my mind, that they need me. And over time, I've come to need them, too."

He paused, waiting for ManMan to respond, so The Man of God did venture to say, "I'm beginning to understand what it means to have people depending on you. It's not an easy thing, is it?"

"No, Mr. . . I'm sorry, I didn't get your name or maybe I did and forgot it."

"Rayford Johnson," ManMan answered, offering the other Mr. Johnson his hand.

"Well, we might be some kin!" They stopped to

look at each other, shook their heads in agreement, and started laughing at the same time.

The guard stifled his laughter long enough to say, "Hey, maybe your daddy or mine one forgot to tell us something 'cause I swear you look like you could be my little brother!" They laughed again.

"But like I was saying, no, it's not easy to have folks depending on you. But you said you were a praying man, right? That's what makes you able to handle it, prayer. Cause if you don't pray, you'll be done walked away from something or somebody God meant for you to help. You'll be done messed up your destiny worrying about what you can and can't handle. And then even worse than that, you'll be done delayed that person's blessing and deliverance. God will still bring them out if they trust Him, but you could have helped them come out a long time ago if you had trusted Him. Does that make sense to you?"

"More than you know," responded ManMan with a twinge of conviction. He was glad he had prayed in the car and that he had not let his fear make him leave without talking to Jerome. But he was totally guilty of leaving home without calling Marie, as he promised he would, and not returning Dr. Barrette's call about his father.

"Well, here we are at the main gate. I'll take you through the first one and Mr. Simon will ask you to see some identification and find out who you come to see when you get to the next one. Now he ain't as cordial as I can be, but don't take offense at him. He's just doing his job the only way he knows how to. Do you know how long you go' be inside?"

"I'm not really sure, probably not more than an hour or two. This is my first visit and I don't know what to expect."

"I just asked because if I'm not here when you come out, I wanted to just tell you it's been good talking to you. You got a good spirit and I felt like you was really listening to me. Whoever you going to see will be glad you came. They all need somebody from the outside to talk to. Not all of them know it, but they all need somebody. So just in case," he said as he offered his hand again, "take care of yourself and be blessed. You can handle it. He wouldn't put it on you if you couldn't . . . Okay, Simon, open this one up. He's ready." He did not give ManMan time to respond before he turned and began the long trek back out to the guard's post in the parking lot. ManMan looked back and watched Isaac Johnson walking away. *Yes, we are brothers, Isaac, we are.*

CHAPTER 19

. . . Thank You for this day, Lord, for my laying down last night and my rising this morning. I bless You, Father, that my bed wasn't my cooling board, nor my cover my winding sheet. I Thank You, Lord, that I didn't receive no bad news this morning when I got up, and that my family is safe and well. I Thank You this morning for my children and their health and strength . . .

It was a prayer Mrs. Johnson had heard for more mornings than she could count. Every morning, rain or shine, good night's sleep or restless, her husband always began their day with a prayer. Over the years, it had begun to sound repetitious. Not because he took God for granted, but probably because she had been hearing it so long. Some mornings she would appreciate being awakened to the sound of her husband's voice talking to God. But there were also some days when she wished he would go in the bathroom to pray or down the hall or somewhere. Today she didn't mind at all. The recent events were causing her to appreciate every moment she spent with him. To be honest, she feared those days might be coming to an end soon. She tried not to think about the possibility of her husband not being there, but her woman-ness, her wife-ness, her mother-ness would not allow her to simply say, "The Lord's will be done." She, like her son hundreds of miles away, was battling with fear.

. . . And Lord, I praise You this morning for my life and my strength. This is the day that You have made and I will rejoice and be glad in it. It's no good that I have done that You have let me live to see this day, but it's by Your grace and Your mercy. God, I just want to say Thank You . . .

His prayer seemed more urgent this morning than it had in many months. Mrs. Johnson realized it as she listened from her side of the bed. Usually she would stay in bed while he prayed, sometimes adding a "Yes, Lord" or a "Bless, Father," but today she couldn't. She got on her knees and faced him on the opposite side. Her heart was weak as she listened to the sincerity of her love's prayer, and although she didn't know it, his was weak, too. The words of the prayer flowed from his very soul. He needed to tell God everything in his heart that he could articulate. Some of the thoughts, feelings, urgings were "groanings that could not be uttered," but those he could find words for, he poured out before the Lord.

. . . My hope is in You, Lord. My faith is in You. I trust You to do what's best, but God, I got some fear trying to take hold of my heart. I know that whatever the outcome of this situation, I'll be good. If You heal me, it will be good. I can stay here and be with my family. If You don't see fit to do it, if that ain't Your will, I'll still be blessed. I'll wake up in Your Presence. But, God, I'm coming as humble as I know how, not asking that You change Your will, but that You give me peace in my heart. I don't know what's best, and You said I can't even think like You, so I'm just asking that You send the Holy Ghost to wrap around me and my family. Comfort us in what we don't know. Help us to rest easy knowing that You know and will do what's best. Help us remember that You never had a case that You lost. Make us to remember that You never had a patient that was beyond Your healing hand, if You saw fit to heal.

As she stood outside her parents' bedroom door, she heard her father's prayers. She knew they would be up by now and was going to go in to say good morning and good bye before she left for class. She had decided she would really stick to it this time. Maybe she would get finished before . . . The thought had been in her head since she found out her daddy had cancer. He might not be there to walk her down the aisle. He might not be there to see his grandchildren. The least she could do was get in school, go full time, take as many classes as she could every quarter, and graduate. It was in her heart to want to believe that he would be healed, that God would indeed work a miracle for the Johnson family. She really did want to believe it. The Word to stand on, she knew. The prayers to pray, she knew. The fasting and laying on of hands, she knew. What she did not know was how to get beyond the fear that was trying to strangle out what she knew to be the reality of God's Promises and Power. All at the same time, each member of the Johnson family was waging a war against the spirit of fear. And neither of them knew if their faith would win.

Jeannine stood listening to her daddy pray like he had every morning since she was old enough to know what prayer was. The phone rang and she rushed to answer it before it rang again. She didn't want it to disturb her father's conversation with God, although neither he nor her mother would have answered it anyway until he was finished and said "Amen."

"Hello."

"Hello, may I speak with Mr. Johnson?"

"I'm sorry, he can't come to the phone right now. Would you like to leave a message?"

"Well . . . do you know when he'll be able to

come to the phone? It is imperative that I speak with him as soon as possible." The voice on the other end of the phone sounded familiar, but Jeannine couldn't quite catch it. She listened intently though.

"He'll probably be available in the next twenty or thirty minutes. Do you want me to have him return your call?"

"Yes, will you please? Can you take this number down?"

"Give me just a minute to get a pencil . . . okay, I'm ready."

"Ask him to call Dr. Barrette's office at 344 – 3366. He can ask to speak with Dr. Barrette or with me, Sanquita, his nurse . . ."

"Girl, I knew I recognized your voice. I just couldn't put my finger on it. This is Jeannine."

"I thought that was you, too, but you know I'm making an 'official call concerning a patient,' so I couldn't just get all loud, Girl. How you doing? I haven't seen you in a while."

"Yeah it's been a minute. I'm back in school, for good this time until I finish. If I had any sense, I would have kept going with you and Shon when we first started. I could have been like ya'll by now – pullin' down that long money."

"Well, I agree that you could have been finished, but I don't know about no long money, Girl. You know I just got married."

"So I heard! My invitation must have gotten lost in the mail . . ."

"Now stop right there. I didn't even send out no invitations. Girl, we saved that money and spent it on the honeymoon. We went the cheap way. You know how they put that line in the newspaper article, 'All friends and relatives are invited through the media. No RSVP required.' You better hear what I'm saying, Honey!"

"You know you've always been a smart girl. I like that about you."

"I'm trying to tell you now. . . But look, give your father the message and tell him he needs to call Dr. Barrette."

"What is it about, San?"

"Now you know I can't tell you that."

"I know. . . But he already told us about the cancer. He told us a while ago."

"I'm so sorry, Girl. I pray he'll be okay . . ."

"Thank, San. Just keep praying. I'll tell Daddy to call the office. He's praying this morning, so I didn't want to disturb him. But I'll stay until he finishes and make sure he calls."

"Okay. Look, we've got to get together soon now, me, you, and Shon. Just for old times sake."

"Hey, wait now, what you mean *old* times sake'? You starting to sound like we're getting old or something."

"You know what I mean. I just really miss it sometimes, you know, the way we used to just hang out together. It was so good, wasn't it?"

"Yes, we did have some good times. Let's try to do something this weekend. I'll call Shon when I get out of class and then call you back, okay? Now we're not go' have to fight your husband, are we?"

"Naw, he can wait 'til I get home. Or he will wait. . . Call me later. For real, Jeannine. I want to do this."

"Okay, I will, I promise."

"Alright. Now let me get back to work before I be at home all the time! I'll talk to you this afternoon."

"Okay, bye."

"Bye."

When she hung up the phone, Jeannine realized that she didn't hear her father praying anymore. She went to her parents' bedroom door and listened for a few seconds. She knocked timidly, not knowing if they were finished praying or had just begin doing so silently. Her mother's voice welcomed her just a quietly as she had knocked, and told her to come on in.

"Good morning, Mama. Where's Daddy?"

"He's in the bathroom. You about to leave for school?"

"Yes, Ma'am. I just wanted to tell Daddy that

Sanquita called and said he should call Dr. Barrett. She said it was really important. Will you tell him . . ." Mr. Johnson's entrance and the towel over his red eyes made her stop mid-sentence. "Daddy, are you okay?" Jeannine's eyes were already beginning to fill with tears, and she had no idea what might be wrong with her father.

"Yeah, Baby, I'm just fine. Just in here talking to the Lord and He got the best of me. You getting' ready to go this morning?"

"Yes, Sir. I was just telling Mama Dr. Barrett wants you to call him. Sanquita said it was important."

Mr. Johnson laughed a deep belly laugh that made Jeannine and her mother look at each other in confusion. "I pray the Lord forgive me," he said between chuckles, "but that boy tickles me. He's so serious all the time, telling me what I should do or what I better do to get well. I thank God for him, but he sho' thinks a lot of his opinion."

"Rayford don't make fun of him. He just cares about you."

"I know it, Baby, but he's still funny. 'Well, Mr. Johnson, I think what we'll do is start you on this new medicine and see how that works out . . .'" His mimicry of Dr. Barrette was amusing and Jeannine and her mother laughed in spite of themselves.

"See how you do, Daddy. Just wait til I see Dr.

Barrette again. I got an appointment in a couple of weeks, and I'm go' make it my business to tell him you been laughing at him."

Mr. Johnson replied to Jeannine as playfully as she had addressed him, "That's okay, but you make sure you tell him his other two patients in this house was laughing at him, too." After he let out another good belly laugh, he said, "Yeah, make sure you tell him that, now."

CHAPTER 20

"Is there anything you want me to tell him? Your name, I mean. Or is he expecting you to come today?" The officer who led ManMan to the waiting room at the prison was cordial, but there was an edge to his voice, too. Maybe without meaning to, he sounded like Clint Eastwood's notorious Dirty Harry character. What a crazy thing for him to be thinking at the time, but ManMan realized it was his nerves causing his mind to stray toward useless thoughts. He was very nervous.

"No, he's not expecting me. You can tell him that the Man of God is here to see him. He'll know who I am." The guard looked at him for a minute, almost said something, but then seemed to think again and turned to enter the final door to the infirmary.

Lord, I don't know what I'm doing, so You got to give me the words to say and when to say them. I don't know what Jerome really expects or wants, but whatever it is, You show me and help me discern in my spirit the real truth behind everything that happens here today. I just want to do right, Father. I want to bless Marie and do the right thing by her, the thing You sent me back in her life to do. I ask that You comfort her in her soul until I can call her or get back to her. I pray for my Daddy, hold him in Your hands and heal him. Thy Will be done. It might sound selfish, Holy Ghost, but I don't want to lose my Daddy this early in my life. I need to keep learning from him how to be a father and a husband and a Daddy. Heal him, Father, in the Name of Jesus, . . .

As he was getting ready to say "Amen," the guard abruptly opened the door again and called him by the name he had sent to Jerome, although he saw ManMan had printed "Rayford Johnson, Jr." in the visitor's log.

"Alright Man of God, Grayson should be ready to see you in a few minutes." There was the slightest air of incredulity in the guard's voice, and ManMan couldn't tell whether it was at "the Man of God" or at something Jerome had said. He quickly settled in his head that it was the latter and replied to the guard.

"Thank you. Should I just wait out here until he's ready or do I need to go in now?"

"You can come on in here now. It's a little waiting area just on the other side of this detector you'll go through." The skepticism had left his voice, and the guard's instructions sounded even and rehearsed. "We have to be careful back in here. Not necessarily of the folks coming to visit, but sometimes the men in here just need one instrument from a supply shelf and we'll all be in a mess. You know everybody that come in here ain't sick."

"Yes, Sir, I can imagine. They get kind of desperate, huh?"

"What you talking 'bout? After they sit in them cells so long, look like just thinking up ways to get out of here, they likely to do or say anything." As they were walking back toward the waiting area on the other side of the metal detector, the guard, J. A. McDonald, as his name tag read, talked to ManMan as if they were old friends.

"This one fellow came in here just holding his stomach and 'bout to fall he was so sick. Or so he claimed. He was just running to the bathroom, said he couldn't hold his bowels, before he could get in the door good, he was in the bathroom. The doctor tried to get him to lay down on the table for his exam, he said he couldn't cause he had to go to the bathroom. The doctor looked at me and I looked right back at him. What was I supposed to do, Man of God?" The guard stopped in the middle of the corridor and reached out to touch ManMan's arm. He, like the other guard, Johnson, wanted someone from the outside to listen. ManMan obliged him and listened as intently as he could. His impending conversation with Jerome weighed heavier on him the closer he got to the waiting area.

"Well, I don't know if there's anything you could have done, short of giving him a dose of Pepto."

"That's what I was thinking, but the doctor saw something I didn't see. He pointed to the inmates pants and saw something hanging out of the back of them. He pointed down, and do you know what I saw? A long strand of toilet tissue. I looked again to make sure I was seeing what I thought I was, and sure enough, there was a long strand of tissue just trailing from behind him. I didn't know what to make of it, and the doctor didn't either. So we just watched him running in and out of the bathroom, watched that trail of tissue get longer and longer. Finally, after about four or five times, I just had to stop him and ask him what he was doing with all that tissue. He looked at me, stopped dead in his tracks, stopped holding his stomach and everything. He straightened up and told me to open the door and let him go back to his cell, and so I did."

He stopped for a moment, seeing the inmate and the tissue again in his mind. "Well," ManMan ventured into his memory, "did you ever find out what he was doing?"

"Man of God, you better believe I asked him

why he come in there acting like he was sick. Do you know what he said? The cots in the cells is real hard and uncomfortable, until you get used to it I guess. He said somebody told him that if he could get them enough tissue paper, they would show him how to get out of prison. So he started trying to figure out where he could get some tissue paper for them. He said he was tired of being shut up in this place. He was getting out of here one way or another, even stuffing his pants with all the tissue in the infirmary bathroom!" McDonald was laughing so hard once he finished that another guard came from the desk in the waiting room to see who was so happy.

"That's one I have never heard before, that's for sure." ManMan was still trying to be engaged in the conversation, but his heart was pounding and his stomach was full of the mutant butterflies. He was scared again. The fear was real. His knees were weak. He knew he was there because God had told him to go. He knew God was there with him. He was not scared because he doubted God: he doubted himself. He had been sent back home to Mississippi and had run away when things got difficult. He had found every reason he could not to stay, and now that same impetus was trying to make him turn around and go back to Atlanta without talking to Jerome. But before he could chicken out on faith, he was standing at the desk in the waiting area filling out the last of three forms required since he entered the prison.

"Do you have any personal items with you?"

"No."

"Do you have any items that could be or would be considered weapons?"

"No."

"Do you have any legal documents that you plan to give to the inmate you are visiting?" This question made ManMan hesitate before he answered. He did have a legal document he wanted to give Jerome, but it wasn't from a lawyer. He wanted to present him with the Word of God and salvation, the two most legally binding elements in the spirit realm.

"No."

"Okay, then, you ready. Just let me call back and make sure Grayson is up to seeing you. He's pretty sick, I guess you know that. Sometimes he wants to see people and sometimes he don't. So far, it's been preachers from around here who come to see all the prisoners who might not have long to live. Is that why you coming to see Grayson, cause he don't have long?"

"Not necessarily. I know he's sick, but I also know him from when we were young. We went to high school together." ManMan stopped there.

He figured that was enough for him to share. He didn't know how much the guards knew and didn't want to betray a trust, although it hadn't really been established yet.

"Oh well that's good. He should be glad to see a friend." The word "friend" hit the Man of God like a hammer. Before now, he had not realized he was perhaps putting himself in the place of being Jerome's friend. Was he really ready for that? Even with all of his conversations with God and his love for Marie and his need to obey what God was telling him to do, was he ready to be a friend to this man? If that's what God had in mind all the time, he would know it soon. The guard hung up the phone and said, "Okay, he's ready to see you."

The room where Jerome's bed was looked long as a football field. ManMan stood at one end and looked down toward the other, thinking about the infirmary his company had redesigned and rebuilt. He had insisted that the infirmary be situated so it didn't look like a hall of death and the dying, which is what this one looked like. The beds were side by side, with too much room between them, and none of them faced one another across the open space down the middle of the room. Instead, they were placed so that each inmate could only look at the wall and not at the person across from him. The nurses and doctors who came to check on the patients were always protected because they didn't have to turn their backs on the patient across the wide, open center space.

Too bad I didn't get a chance to redesign this one. It must be miserable having to stare at a wall all day and all night, if you're well enough to open your eyes and stare at anything. The Man of God tried to think of anything while he was being led to Jerome's bed. It wouldn't take long because there were only seven beds filled. As he passed by five of them, his heart began to beat rapidly. He was scared. Not of Jerome. Not of the prison. Not of the illness that Jerome had or the other illnesses that were wearing thin the bodies of the other inmates in the infirmary. He was scared of what God was going to do to him and through him there in that prison on that day. He didn't know what it was, but he did know it would be miraculous and it would change his life.

"He's been asleep all morning," the attendant tried to offer an excuse for anything Jerome would say or do. "Last night wasn't good for him. He tossed and turned all night his chart says. Are you his brother or a relative?" He whispered like he didn't want to disturb anyone on the corridor.

ManMan thought for a moment, and then answered, "No, not a relative. We went to high school together for a little while. He called me a while back, and I thought I would come and see him today." If only it had been that simple, ManMan's stomach wouldn't be in knots now. But he didn't want to alarm the attendant or to make it seem like anything was awry.

"That's good, Man. He needs somebody to be with him now. I guess you know how sick he is. He's been holding on though, like he's waiting for something. Sometimes when he's full of the drugs and talking out of his head, he'll talk about his life. His wife. A child, a son. Do you know anything about any of that?"

"Yeah, I've heard something about that. But it's been about 20 years since we've really seen each other or talked, before he called me I mean."

"Oh, well I guess you have a lot to catch up on. Let me try to wake him up. He gets kind of feisty sometimes. I just asked him if he wanted to see you. He woke up, sat straight up in the bed and said, 'Yeah, send him on back.' Now look at him, laying there like a log."

"Just take your time. I'm not in a hurry. Don't upset him, let him wake up slowly if he needs to." ManMan was really asking for more time for himself, but he tried not to let on to the attendant.

"Grayson, wake up now, Man. Don't be acting like you sleep. You just sat up in the bed not two minutes ago, so come on and open your eyes.

Jerome Grayson, get up now. You been laying here all morning, somebody done come to see you. Wake up now." Jerome did not respond, but the attendant was not daunted. "Grayson, I'm not go' fool with you now. Get on up. . ." With a wink toward the Man of God, the persistent caregiver said, "Okay, let me tell this pretty women to go on back home. You ain't up to seeing her today."

This must have been a proven strategy because Jerome began to move and stir at the mention of a woman. The male nurse looked over his shoulder at ManMan and whispered, "See, I knew that would work." He moved quickly to help Jerome sit up and put pillows behind him to prop him up. As ManMan stood there watching the attendant prepare Jerome for conversation, he noticed how bad the patient looked. He was barely half the size he was when they were teenagers, which was contrary to the aging process but indicative of the ravages of disease. His face was gaunt and shallow. In certain places on his body, the skin seemed to cover only bones for flesh and muscle was almost absent. The most devastating thing, though, was his eyes. They were dark and empty, with no hope, almost no sign of life.

"Hey there, Rayford, I didn't know you was coming today. But I'm glad to see you." The Man of God heard the words but could not answer. He felt raw, vulnerable, open. But it was not Jerome's appearance that disarmed him. Instead, it was the realization that he was not, could not be mad at Jerome anymore. The cold, bitter, voice on the other end of the phone that had threatened not to tell Marie where her son was, the voice that sounded so evil, was housed in a body that was the most pitiful thing ManMan had ever seen. There was nothing in him that could be mad at Jerome anymore. Regardless of what pain he had caused Marie, this illness and what it had done to Jerome's body was something ManMan would not wish on his worst enemy. Standing there, he felt pity, compassion, and absolute forgiveness.

"Did you hear what I said, Man? I'm glad to see you." Jerome tried to start the conversation again.

"Oh yeah, I didn't really know I was coming today either. I was just sort of led, you know."

"I didn't know who they was talking about. All they said was that a preacher was here to see me. I figured it was one of the ones that come to the chapel every now and then. I didn't even think about you. That's why I was pretending to be sleep. You don't want to tell a preacher you don't want to see him or talk to him, he might give a bad report on you or something. Ain't that right?"

"Well, it doesn't quite work like that I don't

think. We don't generally get asked our opinion. He knows your heart."

"That ain't no better. If The Man Upstairs look at my heart, I'm still SOL. Sorry about that, Man. I'm trying to quit all that cussing and stuff, but you know in here you have to talk a lot of noise and hold your ground. But since I been in here, in the infirmary, it ain't been too bad." He took the slightest pause, stopping suddenly. He was thinking about something else more serious than a cursing problem. As abruptly as he had stopped speaking, he stared again, "Like I was saying, if He know my heart, I'm messed up 'cause my heart ain't worth a damn."

He didn't apologize for the curse word this time. ManMan wasn't offended or anything, so he tried not to make a face or raise his eyebrows or anything that would show discomfort or disapproval.

"Rest assured, Jerome, your heart probably isn't in any worse condition than anyone's is – before they're really changed." He hadn't meant to start sounding like a preacher that soon in the conversation. He figured some small talk would be first, but when God opened the door, the Man of God knew to walk in.

"Changed? Man, I don't think it's enough change in this world to make a difference in me. When you done raised as much hell as I have and messed over as many people as I have, everybody gets tired of trying to deal with you, even that God of yours."

"You'd be surprised how much it would take for Him to get tired of you . . ."

"Is that what this is, laying up here in this bed, sicker than a dog? Is this what happens when He gets tired of somebody?"

"Not at all. I don't think this is a sign of Him being tired of you."

"I'd like to know what it is, then. Can you tell me what it is?" There was the slightest bit of anger in Jerome's voice, but the Holy Spirit was working in ManMan and he was calmer than he had been in a long time.

"I guess the only way I can explain it is to talk about love. His Love. Jerome, when we think about love . . . Wait a minute. Let me ask you before I tell you what I think. When you think about love, what does it mean to you? How do you feel when you think about love?"

Jerome didn't respond immediately, and The Man of God didn't rush him either. They both had nothing but time. Finally, with a timbre of defeated conviction, he did answer.

"To tell you the truth, I can't remember the last time I thought about that. About love. I think the only person who ever loved me, no strings attached, was my son. But it didn't take long for him to figure out what a crazy son of a . . . how crazy I was. Then he was more scared than anything. I didn't do right by him and Marie. I know that. I f'd that up real bad."

"Is Kal'eal really the only person you think ever loved you?"

Another moment of thought preceded the captive's answer. "I guess Marie loved me, too. But I know she *really loved you*. I was just so much, so fast, and she was so young. I really, what do you call it? Like in them old westerns, like Roy Rogers and them? When the dudes in black be hiding behind the rocks?"

"You mean 'ambush'?"

"Yeah, I think I just ambushed her. She walked out of being a smart high school girl to being a wife and mother. I knew I wasn't ready to be nobody's nothing – much less a husband. But I sweet-talked her and kept pushing her and pulling her. Even when I knew she . . . when I knew her heart was full of you. That's why I didn't let her call you. She wanted to – I know she did. But I wouldn't let her. Everything that tied her to Mississippi, I tried to cut loose. The biggest thing was you."

This time it was The Man of God who was silent. He didn't know how to respond. He was being totally disarmed by Jerome's confessions. He never expected the conversations to be this real this early. This depth was for those who swam in the middle of the ocean, not for someone just wading in the water. Jerome must not have sensed ManMan's discomfort, or maybe he was just glad to have somebody before which he could safely lay his burdens. He continued.

"One day she wanted to call you, and I told her she couldn't. Not on my phone. She said, 'Fine, I'll go to the pay phone.' I remember thinking, 'I know she ain't go' disobey me.' Like she was a child or something . . . You know, you don't think about the things you do until they come back on you. One day when they first sent me here, almost five years ago, one of the guards told me to do something. You know me, I was go' do what I wanted to do when I wanted to do it. Guess what he said to me. 'I know you ain't go' disobey me.' Man, that hit me so hard. Then the guard did too." Jerome offered an uneasy laugh, but ManMan could tell that the story was anything but funny to him.

"I don't know how much Marie has told you or if you've even talked with her about me, but I did her real bad, Preacher. When she went to call you that day I told her not to, that was the first time I hit her. She was . . . I mean it hurt her when I hit her, but I think it hurt her more that I actually did hit her. You know what I'm saying?"

"I do. I understand."

"Did you know about any of that? That I used to hit her?"

"She told me about some of it. That's the reason I told God I wasn't going to do anything to help you. I told Him I could die without ever seeing you again. Just as long as you told Marie what you know about Kal'eal."

"So what changed your mind? What made you come up here today?"

"I guess that gets us back to what we started talking about before: love."

"You mean to tell me you came here because you love me?"

"I came here because I love Marie, and the one thing in this world I know she wants more than anything is to know where her child is. And I know you're the only one who knows for sure. So I knew that one way or another, somebody was going to have to come here and talk to you about it. I thought it was going to be a lawyer because I was willing to get you another one if it came to that. Whatever it took. I didn't know God was going to send me, though. My love for Marie is what brought me here."

"So you do still love her, and that much."

"Yes, I do. That's why I had so much anger in my spirit toward you when I first talked to you on the phone. I almost want to say I hated you for everything you did to her. For taking her away from Mississippi, away from home, from her mother, from me. I've never felt that kind of anger toward anybody before."

ManMan's confession to Jerome was just as disarming. Both men just sat there for about five minutes. They were both experiencing something neither of them had expected. Since he was diagnosed with the virus and told there was no cure, Jerome had done a lot of thinking. Most of those thoughts centered around his treatment of Marie and Kal'eal and how he could fix things. He had made that foolish threat about the lawyer because he knew he was helpless. It was a last resort for him. But it had resulted in something he didn't expect – this visit, this conversation with ManMan, who was himself reeling from what God was doing to him and through him. His heart was being totally rearranged. Everything in him was being changed by the Power of the Holy Ghost, the Power of God, the Power of Love. What was the feeling? Did he feel helpless? Scared? Anxious? Whatever it was, The Man of God didn't have time to figure it out or fight it. God was moving in a mysterious way, His wonders to perform.

The attendant came back in the room to check on someone else and noticed Jerome and his visitor were both silent. "Ya'll though talking already? Don't tell me a preacher done run out of words." He wasn't being disrespectful – exactly – but was making an effort at what he thought was humor.

"Man, you just mad ain't nobody coming to see you. Mind your own business." Jerome had an understanding with the attendant and spoke freely.

"Don't trip now, you know I'm the one who distributes your meds, Mr. Grayson. I wouldn't want to mix them up – by accident, of course. Yeah, he's talking big now Mr. Preacher, but just wait til one of them pains hit him." They all laughed at the attendant's exaggerated expressions and imitation of Jerome's reaction to such an "accident."

"See there, even the Preacher laughing. He knows I'm right. But I'll go on and get out of your business. You know I wouldn't do nothing like that. You the only one who gives any good conversation around here. I'm sure you've figured that out by now, Preacher." He knew it was probably being highly judgmental, but ManMan couldn't help but think to himself how effeminate the attendant was. When he finally left the corridor, he was the next topic of conversation.

"Jerome, that attendant is a little bit different, isn't he?"

Before he answered, Jerome laughed a deep belly laugh that came from a genuine place. "Man, you can go ahead and say it. He's as gay as a blade. Everybody in here knows it. You should come around here on Saturday, right before he gets off for the night. I'm talking heels, make-up, tight pants and everything. You would really think he was different then."

"Oh, okay. I'll leave that alone then and go back to what we were talking about before he came in. I think the subject was love."

CHAPTER 21

HER HEART HADN'T ACHED THIS badly since she learned she was pregnant. It was kind of like not being able to breath, but because she didn't pass out, Marie knew she was breathing just fine. She hadn't slept well in the entire three weeks ManMan had been gone from Mississippi. After she talked with Mrs. Johnson, she tried to reach him. Each time she called the office and spoke with someone named Mr. Scott, she refused to leave her name. She had called at least ten times and ManMan was never in the office. Where had he gone? Where was he?

The other person who was, as always, on her mind was Kal'eal. Since she had heard Jerome say he knew where their son was, Marie could hardly keep herself from calling him again. What she didn't want to do was tell him she was on the phone that day, listening to the conversation between he and ManMan. She simply had to talk with Jerome for herself. Perhaps she would say she had just talked with Rayford and that he told her about their conversation. Or perhaps she would just tell the truth. Why should she have to hide the truth from him? He certainly had not worried about playing with her feelings or cared about how much she was hurting. She would call. She would tell him the truth, and, if necessary, beg him to tell her where her son was.

The voice on the end of the line was automated and familiar.

"*What city?*"

"Chicago."

"*What state?*"

"Illinois."

"*What listing?*"

"Illinois State Prison."

"*Please stay on the line for operator assistance.*"

"What listing, Ma'am?"

"Illinois State Prison. I know it's probably not in Chicago, but I didn't know where it was. Can you find the listing for me?"

"Yes, Ma'am, I can search the state listings. It will probably be there. If you hold just a moment, Ma'am. Illinois State Prison. Yes, Ma'am, I have the number. Please hold for the number."

Once she had written it down, Marie stared at the number. All of a sudden, she remembered that she had recorded it before: when ManMan returned

Jerome's first call. She stared at the number. She didn't know how long she held it there, but the phone ringing made her jump.

"Hello."

"Hey, Marie, it's Jeannine. Are you busy? You got a minute?"

"Yeah. What's going on? Is everything alright?"

"Everything is good. Me and Shon and Quita are going to hang out tonight. Why don't you come out with us? Nothing fancy, Girl, we're just getting together. It's been so long."

"That sound like a good idea, Jeannine. I need some good, clean fun in my life."

"Wait now, I didn't guarantee nothing 'bout 'clean,' but you will have fun!" Both women laughed, and both knew that the fun would be good and clean. They had tried it all, been there, done that, and were now fully convinced that was the best kind of fun. No hang-overs. No waking up wondering who was laying beside you. No wondering what they would leave with you.

"What time do you get off work today?"

Marie thought about it and quickly decided to tell Jeannine the truth. "I'm not going in today. I'm taking some vacation days. Some things I need to take care of and try to settle. You know how that can be . . . "

"Yeah, I do. Is anything wrong, Marie? Do you need anything?"

"No, I'll be fine. Just got to do what I got to do. Praying all the way, Girl."

"Well, you know we're all here for you. Me, Mama, Daddy, even that brother of mine. He might not know how to handle it, but I know he still loves you. That's why he went back to Atlanta like he did. You know that don't you?"

"What do you mean? Why did he go back?"

"Because he still loves you, and he doesn't know how to handle it. He's my brother and I thank God for him, but he's not the most expressive man who ever walked the earth. He can think it all in his head, can pray with the best of them, but when it comes to one on one, personal stuff, he's a little slow."

"I know he still loves me. He told me that . . ."

"What? It actually came out of his mouth? Girl, you must be something special!"

"I'm not saying all that, but he did *say* it. And you're wrong about the reason Rayford went back to Atlanta. He went back when he found out something."

"Oh well, that's between you and him, now. You don't have to tell me all of that."

"Naw, I want to tell you. Your mother already knows. I want all of you to know, just in case something does grow between me and Rayford. There's a lot of baggage I brought back to Mississippi with me, and when it all starts coming out, the people who care about me should be ready for it."

Jeannine didn't say anything. She had heard all of the stories and thought she knew everything there was to know about what Marie went through in Chicago. When she didn't answer, Marie kept talking.

"When I left Jerome in Chicago, I just left. You know they took Kal'eal from me. After that, I was so hurt, it was like I was numb. I couldn't feel anything. I started feeling like I feel sometime now – like I can't breathe. After a while I decided I would come home. But I just left. The reason Rayford left was because he found out I'm still married to Jerome." She waited for Jeannine's reaction.

"Oh." What else could she say? Even Jeannine, who prided herself in keeping up with all of the "business" in town, was surprised by this revelation. "Oh, I see."

"I know everybody thought they knew everything, but I didn't even tell Mama that before she died. It was just so much easier to forget Jerome and just let the past be the past. When I came back here, I needed to get myself together first and then try to figure out how to get Kal'eal back. It's been

9 years and the last thing I have thought about is still being married to Jerome. Besides, there wasn't anybody who it would matter to. With all of these 'un-eligible' bachelor's in town."

"I know that's right. I wonder if single men all over the world have as many "situations" as these men around here do. I thought we were the ones who supposed to be suffering from emotional issues, not them."

"You know it." Marie was glad Jeannine lightened the conversation up some. It felt like a risk telling her the real reason ManMan had left, but she was ready to be real with everybody. So anybody, from the mailman to the missionary was vulnerable.

"Have you talked to him since he left?"

"No. I keep calling his office, but he's never there. Or at least that's what the guy keeps telling me. Maybe he just doesn't want to speak to me."

"What guy? Who answers the phone?"

"Somebody named Mr. Scott. Tracy I think."

"He's not there then. If Tracy Scott says my brother is not in, he's not in. Tracy is the only person I know who's never been caught not telling the truth. If ManMan is in the office and he's not taking calls, that's what Tracy will say. He ain't go' tell no lie, now. So is he says that his boss ain't in, you can believe him."

"Oh. Okay."

"I haven't talked to him either. He sends me an email about every other day, but of course I can't tell where he is from that. He didn't say he was going out of town. But now you know I can find out where he is, without much trouble either."

"No, thanks for the offer, but I'm going to give him time to decide what he wants to do. I don't want to crowd him. I still love him, too, but I'm trying to let the Lord handle it. He looked so hurt when Jerome told him we were still married . . ."

"What do you mean when Jerome told him?"

"I didn't tell you that part, did I? When Rayford came home, Jerome called him from prison. He called the office in Atlanta. I guess Mr. Scott called and told him. He told me, and I asked him to call back for me. He came up to the house, and I listened on the other phone. Jerome didn't know I was there, so he acted a real nut with Rayford. Saying he would tell me where Kal'eal is if we got him a new lawyer. He swears he's really innocent this time. A victim of circumstance. They got into an argument and the last thing Jerome said was that he and I were still married. Rayford hung up the phone, said he would call me later and left. The next thing I know, I didn't see his car at the house anymore and he was gone. No call or nothing. That's why I say he left because of that."

"It might not be that, or that by itself anyway. Did he tell you that Daddy is sick?"

"No, what's wrong? Is it anything serious?"

"Yeah, it's cancer."

"Girl, I am so sorry. Is he still going to Dr. Barrette?"

"Yeah, but he said he's not going to take any chemo or anything like that. He doesn't want to get any sicker than he has to trying to get well. Dr. Barrette keeps telling him that the chemo is the best way to go, but you know Daddy. That's where ManMan gets his stubbornness from, and me too, I guess. So your news wasn't the only thing he was dealing with when he left."

"I wish I had known. I never would have gotten him into all this mess with Jerome. Lord have mercy. I wish I had known."

"Now you know my brother, The Man of God. He thrives on this kind of stuff. Nothing ever gets too hard for him, let him tell it. Knowing him, he's sitting at the prison trying to counsel Jerome, get him saved, and find out where your son is all at the same time."

"Girl, I only wish it would work out that way. But that would be too much to ask, even of God."

"Wait now, you what the Word say, 'Is anything too hard for God?'"

"Amen, Madame Bishop!"

"Don't get me started now. You know ministry is already in the family. Do I need to give you a sermon right quick?"

"Come on, Preacher."

"Honey, you know I'm just bluffing. I'd probably run and hide if God told me to preach. I'll sing in a minute, pray at the drop of a hat, teach a class or two, but preaching? Now that takes something the Lord hasn't endowed me with yet."

"Yet?"

"Yet. Leave that alone now. Let's get back to you and trying to figure out whether you want me to find ManMan for you."

"Naw, I don't want you to do that. He'll call when it's time for him to call. In the meantime, I'm going to do what I need to do. I just called information and got the number to the prison. I was sitting here staring at it when you called, trying to get up the nerve to dial it. I just don't know if I'm ready to talk to him."

"Do you want me to pray with you? I can't even imagine how you feel, but I know who does. He knows and He cares."

"Yes, please pray with me."

Father God, in the Name of Jesus, we come to You now just saying Thank You. We Thank You for bringing us to this appointed time and this appointed place. We Thank You for this fellowship and this moment to come to You. God, I lift up my sister Marie to You right now. She needs You now, Father. She needs Your Holy Ghost to come and calm her heart and her spirit. This issue that she's facing now, Father, work it out in her favor. Bring her child back to her arms. Move by Your Spirit and change Jerome's heart. By the Power that only You have, change him, God. Change his whole outlook and attitude, Father. Holy Ghost, go right now to that prison and begin to work a work that no man can explain. Move so strong and so mightily that even he will not understand. And then God, bless my brother. Lift up his spirit and strengthen him. Let him be about Your business even now. In the Name of Jesus. Encourage him. Let him see and do Your Perfect will, God. Bless Kal'eal. Keep him in hope and love. Let him know that his mother loves him and desires to see his face, to hold him in her arms, to love him. Just be God and God all by Yourself. Let Your will be done. We have toiled it seems like all night, God, and have caught nothing. Nevertheless, at Thy Word, we let down our nets again, Jesus. And we expect an abundant harvest. Help us. Hold us. Heal us. In Jesus Name we pray, Amen.

CHAPTER 22

God, I need You to show me how to do this. Their conversation was interrupted by the attendant again because Jerome had to take his medicine. The Man of God took the opportunity to think a short prayer. The conversation was going much better than he thought it would. Actually, he hadn't known what to expect. He just remembered the end of his last conversation with Jerome and how angry they both were. But now, face to face, they were both calm. There was absolutely no tension, no anger, no distrust. All guards were down. *It must be the Holy Ghost. Somebody must be praying for me.* ManMan thought to himself. *Whatever it is, I'm grateful.*

"Look, don't come back in here interrupting our conversation no more. You just trying to be nosy. I still have an hour before it's time to take my medicine."

The attendant didn't answer at first, but Jerome

knew he wouldn't let it pass. "Since you obviously can't tell time, I won't hold it against you," the attendant hissed, "but you've been sleep all day and missed one set of your meds already. I know how to do my job. Excuse me, Mr. Preacher, I don't usually act like this, but this negro right here will make Jesus cuss. Uh oh, did that sound bad? I shouldn't have used the Lord's name in vain like that. I'm sorry, but see what I mean?" He turned back to Jerome and said, "Now you go on and take the rest of this medicine."

ManMan sat and watched as Jerome emptied each of the six small white cups' contents in his hand and then in his mouth. He wondered what they all were. There were at least two pills in each cup, some of them holding four or five. It seemed like so much medicine for one body to handle, but it was only one in a series of daily doses, as the attendant had said.

When he was finished swallowing the pills and chasing them down with water, Jerome added one last quip, "I tell you what, you don't come in here no more unless I call you. How about that?"

"Oh don't worry, Honey, cause I am off for the afternoon. I have some business I need to take care of outside these walls. By the way, Milfred said somebody called you a few minutes ago. A woman." Over his shoulder, the attendant couldn't help but try to have the last word, "You've been keeping secrets from me, huh?"

"See there, I told you he was nosy." Jerome spoke to ManMan again, but he was wondering who had called him this time of the day. Usually his mother would call, but always in the evening after his sisters had come to pick their children up. She was their free baby-sitting service, but she didn't mind. "As long as my body can keep up with them, I don't mind," she would always tell Jerome when he told her she needed to make his sisters take the kids to daycare.

"Hey, Milfred." Jerome yelled and caused ManMan to jump in spite of himself. "I'm sorry 'bout that, Man. I just want to find out who this was calling me in the middle of the day. Mama calls, but always in the evening. I hope ain't nothing wrong with them . . . Hey, Milfred." He yelled again and then was silent, waiting for a response.

"Grayson, I know that ain't you hollering at me like that. You must be trying to show out in front of the Preacher," Milfred yelled back. "What you want? The ward must be on fire the way you hollering. What you want? You know I can't leave this post." Now Milfred was silent waiting on Jerome's reply.

"I'm just trying to find out who called me.

Sweet said somebody had called me since Rayford been here. Who was it?"

"I don't know. Didn't sound like your Mama, though. This was a young woman. I ain't never heard that voice before."

"Did she leave a name or anything?" From the look on his face, ManMan could tell that the yelling was hurting Jerome's throat or causing him some kind of discomfort. He didn't interrupt because he didn't have the rapport with Milfred that Jerome did.

"Do you want me to go see if there's a message?" he offered Jerome, "I can go see if he took a message. Don't yell anymore. Seems like it hurts. I'll go." Before Jerome could catch his breath and answer him, ManMan was on his way down the hall to the desk he had passed earlier. The officer sitting there had barely looked up at him. ManMan wasn't apprehensive though. God was doing something so whatever happened would be fine.

"The restroom is around the corner, no vending machines on this floor, only in the officers' area. You can make a phone call if you need to, but long distance calls must be charged to a credit card or a calling card." Milfred stopped talking as abruptly as he had started. When ManMan did not move immediately, the guard finally looked up from his newspaper and asked, "Is there something else you need?"

"Yes, as a matter of fact, Mr. Grayson sent me to see if there was a message from the phone call he received. If so I'd like to take it to him."

After a moment of thought, Milfred finally answered, "Well, I'm not supposed to give out information like that to anyone but the inmate it's for, but since you're in there visiting him, I guess I can give it to you. You can't very well go too far with it." But just in case, the guard carefully removed the message from the pad and folded it twice. He then reached into the drawer and pulled out an envelope, into which he put the message. Only after sealing the envelope as carefully as he had folded the message did Milfred finally give it to the Man of God.

When he arrived back on the ward, Jerome's eyes were closed. He was still propped up on the pillow, but his head was resting in the lock of his shoulder, and ManMan didn't know whether to wake him or not. He decided against it and sat down quietly in the chair beside the bed. He turned the envelope over and over in his hand while he waited for Jerome to wake up or stir or open his eyes or something. His mind began to wander back to Mississippi and Marie. He had a sudden urge to call her and tell her where he was. Surely she would understand and be glad and forgive him for having not called since he'd left home. He also wanted to call his father and ask how he was doing. But he would definitely have to wait until Jerome woke up again. The last thing The Man of God wanted was for Jerome to think he was not serious, or was talking a game he wasn't fully committed to playing.

"Man, you should have woke me up," Jerome opened his eyes embarrassed and surprised he'd fallen asleep so quickly. "You should have shook my foot or called my name or something. It could have been the rest of the day and I'd have still been asleep."

"It's all good. I was about to crawl in that bed over there and get me a nap, too." They both laughed at the thought. "They must sleep mighty good if you just dozed off like that. I wasn't gone but two or three minutes." As he spoke, ManMan handed the envelope with the phone message in it to Jerome, who looked at it strangely, wondering why the envelope was necessary. "He said it was really against the rules to give the message to anybody but you, so he sealed it up in the envelope."

"Milfred need to quit trippin'. He tells more of other folks' business than they can tell themselves. He need to quit." Jerome started to open the envelope then, as an afterthought wanting to show

ManMan trust was not an issue, he passed the envelope back to its carrier and said, "Go ahead and open it. Milfred act like it's some big CIA case or something. It probably ain't nothing but Mama done called with the latest emergency from FeFe and them. She keep letting them upset her over nothing. Then she calls me like I can really do something. I guess she just needs somebody to talk to. Somebody who'll really listen. Everybody need that sometimes."

His words trailed off into silence and ManMan took the opportunity to open the envelope and read the message. Jerome watched in silence and waited to receive whatever information Milfred had recorded. When ManMan didn't speak immediately, Jerome's continence changed. He figured from the way The Man of God was staring at the paper, it must have been something really serious or really bad.

"What is it? It's something bad, ain't it? I can tell from the way you looking. Is it my Mama? Is she alright?"

Without really realizing it, ManMan held up his hand to stop Jerome from speaking. After another beat and when he had come to himself, he looked straight at Jerome. "It's Marie. She called. And she's on her way here."

CHAPTER 23

"Good morning, Sir, how are you?"

"I'm doing alright, Doctor, how you feeling this morning?"

"Things are going well this morning, Mr. Johnson . . ."

"Well that's good to know that *things* are going well, but I asked how *you* are doing."

"Yes, Sir, you got me on that one. I'm doing fine." Dr. Barrette allowed the slightest moment of silence and then dove in head first. "Mr. Johnson, did you think about what we discussed last week? We really need to start the treatment as soon as possible. I think we'll have the best results if we begin now . . ."

Mr. Johnson cut Dr. Barrette off before he went any further, "Okay, Son, I'll start the treatment."

"Are you serious, Mr. Johnson?"

"Yes, I'll start the treatment as soon as you guarantee it will save me. That I'll live through it and then be healed after it's done. Can you do that? Is that a promise you can make me? Can you give me that for sure?" From the silence that followed he knew he had taken his surrogate son by surprise with the sharpness in his voice, but he wanted the young doctor to finally hear him and understand that no meant no. To ease the tension of the moment, Mr. Johnson began again. "Listen Son, I'm not trying to be cold or anything, and God knows I trust you more than I have any doctor in all my life, and I've known two or three others, have had operations, and the whole bit. I trust you and I love you like my own son. Now I need you to trust me. I don't know what God is going to do. Will I live or will I go home to be with Him from this cancer? I do not know, Son. But whatever happens, I'm going to let Him have control. Like I told you before, I've seen what them treatments can do to somebody. They get sicker than they are, they lose they hair. Not that it will matter in my case." He offered an uneasy laugh, without response from the Doctor. "I know your tests and things say I should take the chemotherapy and make the best of it. I know you're the doctor and you're offering the best advice you know how to. I know all of that. But Doc, I'm telling you now and for the last time: I'm not taking the treatments. Not now, not ever. I won't do it."

"Yes, Sir, I hear you, and I won't bother you about them again. Will you still be coming in for your appointment next week?"

"Yes, I'll be there."

"Okay, that's good. I'll tell my nurse to call and remind you a couple of days before."

"That'll be good, but you know my wife won't let me forget. We'll be here."

"Yes Sir. Have a good day, and I'll see you next week."

"Alright, Son, I'll see you then. Goodbye."

"Goodbye."

When Marie found out that the ticket to Chicago would be over a thousand dollars, she regretted having called and left Jerome the message that she was coming to see him. She didn't have a thousand dollars just laying around. Her savings account was only about five hundred, and if she cashed in one of her 10 or so CDs, the penalties would be ridiculous. She could do a short term loan at the credit union but that would take up to a week to approve. She needed to go now – before she lost her nerve, before she had time to think about what she was doing, about the chance she was about to take . . .

Packing was always a chore for her, but Marie was oddly focused as she got ready to leave for the prison. Strange, especially since she still hadn't figured out how to pay for her trip. She felt a tremendous peace about the whole thing. Maybe it was because she had finally decided to do something. For the last 9 years she had been tormented by thoughts of where her child might be, how he might be suffering, might be thinking that she had abandoned him and wondering why she had not come to rescue him.

Win, lose, or draw, she was going to finally do something. Would Jerome tell her where Kal'eal was? Would he see her? Had he even gotten the message? Despite all the questions and the things that could possibly go wrong, Marie kept packing because one way or another, this was a trip she would take.

All of a sudden, she remembered what Rayford's mother had told her, ". . . *If you need . . . some money . . . all you have to do is ask.*" Marie hoped she was serious.

"Hello, Mrs. Johnson, this is Marie."

"Hello, Baby, how are you this morning?"

"I'm fine. Mrs. Johnson, you know when we were talking and you said if I ever needed anything, I should ask?"

"Yes, I remember that. And I meant it, too. Do you need something?"

"Yes Ma'am. I'm going to see Jerome. He's the only one who knows where my son is and I need to find out. That means I need to go to the prison. But . . ."

"Well, I know you're going to have to fly. The drive would be too long to make by yourself. You're going to go right away aren't you?"

"Yes Ma'am, that's what I was trying to do, to leave early in the morning."

"Okay, so the ticket is probably what, about a thousand dollars? How much of that do you have? Do you need all of it? If you do, that's not a problem."

"Thank you, Mrs. Johnson, that's what I was calling for, to ask if I could borrow some money. I have about five hundred dollars in my savings account, but the ticket is a little bit more than a thousand. I can get that out and . . ."

"No, don't bother your savings, Baby, you'll need that for something else. Let me get myself together and I'll have that for you. Do you want me to bring it to you or will you come by here and pick it up? I can drop by your house on the way from the bank."

"No Ma'am, I wouldn't ask you to do that . . ."

"You're not asking, I'm offering."

"Yes Ma'am, but I can come to the house to get the money. And I'll pay you back some every month when I get paid. It will take some time but I will pay you back."

"I know it, Sweetheart. I know you will. Let me call you when I get back home, okay. It'll be sometime after twelve, but if I miss you, just come on by anyway."

"Mrs. Johnson, I . . . I . . . I . . ."

"Don't worry about it, Baby, I know it's a good investment. And I know you're grateful. Just go and do what you need to and find your child. He deserves to know you, and you deserve to have him, to raise him, to love him. I'll call you when I come from the bank. Bye-bye."

"Bye, Mrs. Johnson and thank you."

She didn't know if Mrs. Johnson heard her or not, but she was truly thankful. Her heart couldn't contain all of the emotions she was feeling, and Marie soon found herself looking for something to wipe the tears from her face so she could finish packing.

God, I just bless You for Your favor. Even when I don't know how, You've already made it so, You've already been there and done what I need done. I bless Your Name, Jesus, and I lift and magnify You above every fear and every doubt. I know that You have not given me a spirit of fear, but of love, of power, and of a strong mind. I claim what's already in me, Father. As I go to face I don't know what, I go in the faith that You've already been there, that You are already there for me. Hallelujah! And Father, I pray a special blessing on Mrs. Johnson, on her whole family, on her children, and on her husband, God. Every way You can find to show them favor, do it. Every miracle You can see to work for them, just work them. Whatever You see them standing in the need of, God, for the blessing they are to me, provide for their every need according to Your riches in Glory . . .

. . . According to Your Will, Father, I'm going through this and I don't know how it's go' end up. I care about what's going to happen, but I know You've got it all in Your hands. I feel good, my body ain't hurting, and I'm go' try to make the best of it. Give me the strength I'm go' need, but more than that, give my doctor what he needs. Help him to understand that I do trust him, but I trust You more. Let him know I ain't trying to be hard-headed or to die before my time. Speak some comfort to him, as a doctor, as him being just like my son. Comfort him, God.

Mr. Johnson had been praying by himself this time, and he knew his spirit was encouraged and at ease, but his natural man was fighting an encroaching fear. Not of the disease or the process he might go through because of it, but because of the effect it might have on his family. He knew that his beautiful, faithful wife of many years put up a good front, but she was fragile in so many ways. The first time one of her children was in the hospital, when Jeannine fell out of the swing at school and broke both of her forearms, Rayford, Sr. realized just how vulnerable his wife could be.

When the teacher called her at work, Mrs. Johnson was calm and made two calls from her desk. She called her husband and she called the school to tell the office not to put ManMan on the bus. His aunt would come and pick him up. She knew her son wouldn't be alarmed because his Aunt Hattie often served as a stand in baby sitter/carpooler/errand runner for her. By the time Mr. Johnson got to the hospital, Jeannine had already been moved from the emergency room upstairs to have her arms x-rayed. The doctor's wanted to make sure that there were only "regular" breaks before they set the bones and caste her arms.

He found his wife sitting in the waiting room staring at the wall. From the way she looked, he wondered if it was just broken bones they were dealing with or something worse. He remembered thinking that he had never seen her look so pitiful, so helpless, so much in shock as she looked in that moment. His heart fell to his feet as he went to her side and asked, "What did the doctor say?" Without saying a word, Mrs. Johnson looked at him and within the blink of an eye, she was crying in his arms like Jeannine had not survived her accident. "Baby, what is it? What did the doctor say? Is she go' be alright?" She nodded her head as it lay on his chest and he felt some relief. But her heavy, uncontrollable tears still bothered him. "Well why you crying so hard? She go' be alright. They just go' put some castes on and she'll be alright. Hey, calm down now. It's go' be okay." Despite his words of comfort, the mother's tears only got heavier. She cried for a solid twenty or thirty minutes, and all he could do was hold her in his arms.

Just as he had assured her, Jeannine was fine and her arms mended without incident. Soon she was back at school full time and back in the swing, although she never tried jumping out of one again. Mr. Johnson knew the pain and discomfort her child's accident had caused those many years ago was nothing compared to what his death would bring to his wife's heart and soul. So he prayed more for her and less for himself as the days went by . . .

CHAPTER 24

THEY BOTH JUST SAT THERE in silence, neither really searching for what to say as much as what to feel. Jerome didn't know if he was scared or sick because his stomach was all of a sudden turning cartwheels. ManMan's mind was in overdrive. He wanted to say something but no words would come. They wouldn't come because his spirit man had already taken over. He was already praying in his prayer language in his head. No English or natural words were flowing. Instead, the prayer tongues he had been baptized in and endowed with at the age of 25 were flowing like a river. He wanted to say "Excuse me" or "I'll be back" or something before he left, but he simply couldn't. He knew that if he opened his mouth, the only sound that would come out was that of his spirit making intercession. He didn't want to alarm Jerome, so he just got up and left the corridor.

Jerome summoned all his strength and sat up.

He swung his legs out of the bed. For what? Did he need to get "ready?" How ready could he get? He could change into a clean hospital gown and put on the hand-me-down robe that had been issued to him. But wait. He wasn't even sure when Marie was coming. Had she even left or was she just calling to tell him that she was coming? Did the note say "I'm on my way" or "I'm coming to the prison" or "I'm coming to see you" or "I'll be there in a few days." He looked toward the end of the bed to see if the note had been left there by The Man of God. Not there. He was tired from just sitting up and dragging his legs to the side of the bed, but he had to find the note. He struggled with all of his strength to stand up and shuffle to the chair where his visitor had been sitting. There it was. Laying there just as it had been taken out of the envelope, folded over once.

He was surprised at how badly his hand was shaking when he picked it up. He tried to convince himself that it was because he was so weak. It wasn't much of an effort and Jerome let himself be resigned to the fact that he was just scared. He thought he was ready to confront or to be confronted by Marie. His days and nights were often spent rehearsing what he would say to her when they finally did meet face to face. Now that the moment might actually be approaching, the man was scared. Nothing, not his life on the streets, not his near fatal brushes with death, not his diagnosis of HIV, nothing had ever put this kind of fear in him.

In Jerome's mind, Marie held a key for him. He knew that if he ever really had a chance to make things right, to get right with God, he had to have Marie's forgiveness. He had to somehow find the words to ask her to release him from the guiltiness he had surely earned. That's why he had called in the beginning. Even after he called, his pride took over and he didn't just say, "Hey, tell Marie I'm sorry and I want to tell her that face to face. I want her to know where her son is." No, he had to call with a threat, trying to have the upper hand. He knew there was no way in heaven or hell he would ever get out of jail alive. Still, he tried to draw ManMan and Marie into a foolish game of give and get. How could he have been so stupid – again? How could he hope she would ever forgive him?

The note was as simple as The Man of God had made it seem. "Somebody named Marie called and said she coming to see you. She didn't leave no number, just said she was coming." That was it. Just that simple. That's all Milfred had written, so Jerome was right back where he started – not sure when Marie would be there. He looked toward the doorway to see if ManMan was coming back. No sign. He wondered where he had gone and thought about trying to make it to the door, but the few steps it had taken to get him to the chair at the end of the bed were almost enough to wipe him out. He knew he'd never make it to the door by himself. Thankfully, as the realization of how weak he was set in, The Man of God showed up in the doorway. He quickened his steps when he saw that Jerome was out of the bed and leaning heavily on it, to steady and keep himself upright.

"Hey, should you be out of bed?" ManMan asked in a scolding tone as he put Jerome's arm around his shoulder and literally put him back in the bed. His effort seemed to shock the patient, who did not resist or refuse the help. He was thankful for the lift.

"I thought I was go' have to come and get you, the way you left out of here without saying anything. You done made me get up out the bed when I don't even do that to go to the bathroom." He chuckled uneasily. "Where did you go anyhow?"

"Just down the hall. I had to get myself together. The note really surprised me. I haven't talked to Marie since I left from down home three or four weeks ago . . ." Before he knew it, ManMan had let on that he had been in Mississippi when Jerome first contacted the office and that he had talked to Marie.

"So you were there when I called your office

and they called you? I thought I felt something when I talked to you that day. Were you actually there with her when you called me back?"

After a moment of thought, ManMan decided since Marie would be there soon and the truth had to come out anyway, he wouldn't hold anything back. "Yes, I was at her house when I called you back. The first thing I did was tell her you had called and asked if she wanted me to call you back. She said yes and told me to make the call while we were there together. She was on the other extension. She heard everything you said . . ."

"Damn. So my big mouth just got me further in, didn't it? I guess she does want to come up here now, since she knows you're here and all . . ."

"That's just the thing," said the Man of God with the slightest hesitation, "she *doesn't know I'm here*. I have no idea why she decided to come. When I found out you were still married to her, I just left."

"Why? I know you didn't think she still loved me or nothing like that. After all I did to her and all the pain I caused her, I know you didn't think that me being married to her still meant something."

"I don't know what I was thinking. All I could think was that she had somehow deceived me . . ."

"Wait. Stop right there. I know this may not mean anything coming from me, but the last thing Marie would ever do was try to mess with anybody like that. I mean all the time we were together in Chicago, no matter what I did or how bad I treated her, she always did what she was supposed to do. You know one time I had beat her so bad I needed somebody to kill me, to put me out of my misery. I came in that evening and asked her where my food was. She had left it on the table. When I sat down to eat, she knocked the plate off the table. Of course, my dumb ass beat her again. But you know why she knocked it on the floor? The girl across the hall gave her some kind of poison or something and she put it in my food. All she had to do was sit there and watch me eat it. She would have been out, free. But she risked another beating to save my sorry ass. That's the kind of woman she was then, and I know she ain't changed that much. That's why I know if she didn't tell you about us still being married, it wasn't to try to fool you or anything. She wouldn't do nothing like that. She's a good woman."

The Man of God didn't know how to respond or if he needed to respond. Jerome possessed more wisdom and truth at that moment than the Preacher ever had. For a while they sat in silence again, each trying to work through the emotions they were feeling and the uneasiness Marie's impending visit had begun to foster in their spirits. They were both afraid of the retribution their actions would undoubtedly engender. ManMan had left

Mississippi without a word and hadn't called since he'd been gone. When Mr. Scott gave him the messages that Marie had called, he acted like he was too busy to return her calls. He had been foolish and would surely have to face her in the light of his foolishness when she got to the prison. He reasoned that she would probably not be there today or before he left, so he would have time to get his "speech" together.

Jerome was facing a different kind of fear altogether. It was rooted in the many times he had beaten Marie. The many names he had called her. The many days she had lived in fear of him, his temper, and his heavy hands. The many nights she had cried herself to sleep because she wanted so badly to talk to her mother on the phone. The many times he had told her that she was nothing and would never be anything without him. The years she had been without her son. He knew there was much for which he had to repent, and only Marie could serve as true priest and hear his confession – for it was she who had endured the most suffering because of his sins. Not sure how it would work out, Jerome became more and more restless as the moments ticked by.

The plane ride had been more restful than she thought and before Marie knew it, she was at the airport in Chicago. The steward tapped her gently on the shoulder after all the other passengers were off the plane.

"Ma'am, were in Chicago." His voice was kind and seemed to regret that he had to wake Marie from such a peaceful nap. "You must have been really tired, Ma'am, you missed your in-flight meal and everything. I don't think you stirred at all."

"I'm as surprised as you, but I guess the Lord knew I needed some rest. This trip is one I've been dreading for a long time . . ."

"Yes, Ma'am, but sometimes you just have to do what you have to do . . . Did you have anything in the overhead compartment? I'll be happy to get it for you."

"Yes, there is a small black bag with the initials MAC on it. It should be right over my head."

He took no time at all securing the bag and helping Marie get herself together before she went into the airport. "Is someone meeting you here or do you have to go to them?"

"I guess you can say I have to go to them. Or him. He can't come to meet me right now. Not that I'd really want him to . . ."

Not fully understanding what she meant, the steward didn't question Marie anymore. He must have realized that this conversation was headed in a direction his thirty minute layover would not accommodate, what with taking a real restroom break, getting something to eat, and calling home. He let his training kick in and said, "Well, I hope you've enjoyed your flight and that your stay in Chicago is just as enjoyable. We look forward to seeing you again."

The airport was huge, and Marie tried to act like she knew where she was going. The first thing she had to do was find the luggage belt and then the car rental counter. Although she had reserved a vehicle before she left, the line she faced after she got her suitcase threatened a shortage. She prayed, *"Lord, don't let them run out of cars before I get up here. I need to get on the road to the prison before I change my mind and go back to Mississippi. Just let the cars last until I get up there and get mine. By Your Spirit, Father.*

"May I help whose next in line?" The medicine Mr. Johnson was taking for high blood pressure hadn't changed for years. Dr. Barrette was always monitoring it. Until the cancer was discovered, Mr. Johnson's blood pressure was the priority. The line at the drug store wasn't too long but was moving unusually slow. It felt like he had been standing there for hours. His cell phone's ring still shocked Mr. Johnson, but when he was in public he tried to act accustomed to it. He looked at the screen to see who was calling. "My Baby" showed up and he smiled in spite of himself.

"Hey Baby, where are you?" His wife's sweet voice could soften life's harshest blows.

"I'm at the drug store trying to pick up my pills. The line kind of long, but I hope it won't be too much longer. Did you need me to bring something home with me?"

"Naw, I just wanted to let you know that I took some money out of the bank . . ." Her hesitation made him wonder how much and what the emergency was. They had built an understanding and trust about everything during the many years of their marriage, especially money. Unless the amount was large, she needn't tell her husband every little amount of money she spent. For years she had worked and put her money in their joint bank account. They had never even considered having separate ones. "If you can't trust a person with money, you sho' don't need to be sleeping in the same bed with 'em," Mr. Johnson would always say. He knew that if she called him and didn't wait until he got home to tell him, the amount had to be significant.

"What happened? Is everything alright?"

"Yeah, it's just that Marie wanted to go to Chicago to see Jerome in prison, to try to find out where her child is, and she didn't have enough money to get the ticket. I took out $2,000 and gave it to her. I went in the savings account . . ." She stopped again, and even though she knew he would support her, Mrs. Johnson didn't want it to sound like she was doing things without considering her companion first. After all, he had contributed as much money to their emergency fund as she had.

"Well, Baby, that's okay. That's what it's for — emergencies. She needed it and she just like one of our children. That's just fine. Did you tell her she didn't have to worry about paying it back? It'll be okay if we don't get it back. You know we told her mama we'd take care of her and help her when she needed it."

"I'm glad you said that. I was thinking the same thing."

"Did she go by herself?" asked Mr. Johnson with the honest concern of a father. "I wish she'd have called Rayford, Jr. to go with her or somebody."

"You know I think she did go by herself. That son of ours hasn't called her since he left from down here. I don't think she wanted to bother him since he was acting kind of funny like that."

"She don't need to worry about that. He ain't called me since he left either, and I'm his daddy. I could tell her don't worry 'bout that. That's just the way he act sometimes. She can't take it personal."

"I know, Baby. You know I know how he can be. I guess he's still in Atlanta. He hasn't sent Jeannine any emails for a couple of days now."

"He'll call soon. He just got to work through things. He'll call."

"You got another call, Grayson. I guess you the most popular man in stir today." Milfred came in the ward this time to deliver the message himself. Sealing the note up in an envelope to send it to Jerome was too much trouble. "They don't pay me to be your secretary. I guess you go' have to ask the warden to get you your own extension by the bed or something. Here the message. It's from your mama."

What else could happen, Jerome thought to himself. He wanted to give the note to ManMan this time, too, but he want ahead and read it. What could be more of a shock than Marie being on her way to the prison? After that, he could take anything.

Your Mama said to call her. She need to talk to you as soon as you can.

"Milfred, can I come use the phone?" He knew it would take Mildred a while to answer. Not that he didn't hear, but he just always chose when – or if – he wanted to respond.

ManMan offered to go ask him, but Jerome silenced him by holding up both of his hands. He began to do a silent count down, using his fingers as the unofficial timekeepers. . . . *Three, two, one.*

"I guess you can come use the phone. It was

your mama and it sounded important. You know I don't do this for nobody else, just let 'em use the phone anytime they want to. But it sounded important, so you can come on."

The journey to the telephone was arduous. With each step Jerome felt like his bones were disconnecting themselves at the joints. The Man of God walked with him, which, at first the prisoner resented and resisted. By the time they got about half way the corridor, though, ManMan was bearing most of Jerome's weight and walking for the both of them. "You need to stop and rest? You can sit here on the bed if you need to. Or I can go ask for the phone and bring it to you."

His pride wanted to say he could make it without resting or that he didn't need the phone to be brought to him, but either statement would have been a lie. "Yeah, let me sit down on this bed for a minute. If you feel like getting your feelings hurt, you can ask Milfred if you can bring me the cordless phone. He guards that thing like it's his cell phone and he ain't got no daytime minutes left. You can ask him, but I know what he's probably go' say . . ."

Once he settled Jerome on the side of the borrowed bed, ManMan went to the desk and asked for the phone. He braced himself for a harsh "No," and was surprised when Milfred held the phone out to him and said, "All he had to do was ask for it in the beginning." With that, he disappeared behind the newspaper he had been reading since ManMan went in to visit Jerome.

"Hello, I'm here to pick up a vehicle. I reserved it over the internet, and I printed out the confirmation. Do you need to see that?"

"No, Ma'am, if you can just tell me the name the reservation is held in, I'll be glad to check availability for you." *Check availability?* The words made Marie's heart beat faster. Although she had prayed about it and the line had moved quickly, she was still anxious that there were no more cars left. She had seen it so many times from the other side of the counter when she worked at the airport for three years. The airlines would overbook flights and then when people showed up to get on the plane, there would be no seats for them. She had to admit that many times she didn't care whether or not people had seats. If she had known then what she knew now . . .

"I'm sorry, Ma'am, but we don't have any more cars in the size you reserved. You reserved a mid-size and all we have left are luxury vehicles. I can offer you one at no additional cost to you or I can try to book you with another company . . ." The young woman at the desk was about to continue, but Marie's smile told her she didn't need to.

"I take it that the upgrade is fine with you?"

"Yes, it's just fine." *Thank You, Jesus. Yes, Lord, You don't just answer prayer, but You go above and beyond. Thank You, Jesus.*

Thank You, Jesus, for a good husband. He's so good to me, Father, and I'm grateful to You for him. After she hung up the phone, Mrs. Johnson reminded herself of just how blessed she was to have had so many rich years with her husband. They hadn't always had everything she thought they needed, but never had there been a time or place when she felt her husband hadn't tried to provide the best. She never had to run him down in the streets, never had to wonder where his money was going, never had to fuss and argue with him about how to discipline the children. Theirs was a marriage to model after. Now he was possibly going to get sick, sicker than she could even imagine, and she didn't know if she was ready to handle it. If the shoe had been on the other foot, she had no doubt her husband would have never batted an eye at the possibility of waging a battle with cancer right beside her. But she feared in her spirit – that she might not be able to handle it . . . that she might let him down.

The "luxury vehicle" was just that and didn't let Marie down a bit. She hadn't packed a lot and had as much traveling room as she needed. The internet directions said the trip would take about two and a half hours, but she knew in actual time, it would probably be much less. She could always shave off at least forty-five minutes. This time she might use all of it while she tried to rehearse what she would say to Jerome. *"Look, I didn't come to argue with you or to accuse you of anything. I don't need any apologies. All I need is for you to tell me where my child is."* That sounded really good, but she knew Jerome wouldn't let it be that easy. He would probably try to strike up a conversation about something else altogether, probably this fool idea of getting another lawyer and getting out of prison. Or about the marriage. Or about how much she owed him. Or some other foolish thing.

"Hello?"

"Hello, Mama, this Jerome. You called up here?"

"Yes, I called 'bout fifteen minutes ago. I didn't expect them to let you call back this evening."

"Is anything wrong? Milfred said you said it was important. Is something the matter?" Jerome held his breath waiting for some word of a death or an incident with one of his sisters and their children.

"Naw, ain't nothing really wrong. I just called to tell you that we'll be up there this weekend. I know we got to wait until the weekend to come see you. We'll be there this weekend."

Jerome thought to himself that this was hardly

an emergency. It had been two months since his mother had come to see him so he was expecting she would make the trip soon. "Mama, I figured you would be coming soon. Is that all you wanted to tell me? I thought something was wrong from the message you left."

At first she didn't respond and Mrs. Grayson felt the lump in her throat get bigger. She knew what she had to say and do was absolutely necessary and unavoidable. Still she was nervous, maybe even scared. "That ain't all I called to tell you . . ."

Jerome let the silence stand as he waited for the other shoe to drop. "What is it, Mama? Go ahead and tell me whatever it is. I'll be alright."

"Well, I'm not coming by myself. I'm bringing the boy with me. He need to see you before it's too late. You need to tell him what happened, tell him about his mama. Every time I look at him, growing older and getting ready to be a man, I know in my soul we can't keep the truth from him no more. He need to know. I know you asked me not to tell him nothing, and I ain't told him nothing. It ain't for me to tell him. But come hell or high water, I'm bringing him up to the prison and you go' tell him. Do you hear me? Do you understand what I'm saying?"

The sudden boldness she felt was strange to Mrs. Grayson. She had always, according to her daughters, "spoiled Jerome like he was Jesus or somebody." Perhaps she had. Maybe that was why he turned out like he did. Whatever the reason and regardless of what mistakes she had made with him, she was determined that her grandson would have the chance at something different. She told herself she should have called Marie as soon as Jerome went to prison, but she tried to hold out hope he wouldn't stay long. After three or four years passed, she was so ashamed she couldn't muster up the courage to call. Now, with the very real possibility her son wouldn't live another year in or out of prison so heavy in her spirit, Mrs. Grayson decided she would give Jerome one chance to tell Kal'eal the truth. If he refused, she would do it herself and she would call Marie and tell her to come get her son.

He was all that was on her mind now. When she decided to go to the prison and confront Jerome in person, she didn't really think about the after effects of her visit. If he refused to tell her about Kal'eal, she would have to try to go through legal channels. If he told her . . . another horrifying thought came up in Marie's spirit: what if Jerome didn't know anything after all? What if the social workers had put him in the "system" and Kal'eal was just floating around from foster home to foster home? The last time she called, about a year ago, the only thing they would tell her was that "Kal'eal Grayson has been placed in the care of family members." Because since she was not the "custodial parent" according to court records, the case worker wasn't supposed to share information with Marie. Under threat of losing her job, the voice on the other end of the line had whispered only one hint: "You should try his father's side of the family."

And she did just that. She called the last number she had for Jerome's mother. It was disconnected. Both of his sisters' addresses changed as often as the weather, and they didn't believe in keeping telephones in their names. Marie had called any and everybody who might know how to contact Jerome's family except Jerome. Until ManMan came back into her life, she didn't think she would ever have the strength or the courage to talk to the man whom, although he was still her husband, was the one person she had ever hated in this world. That's why when the guard, she thought she remembered that he said his name was Milfred, asked her if she wanted to speak with Jerome before she came to the prison, she said no, asked him to deliver the message, and quickly hung up the phone.

The cell phone ringing was a surprise because he was sure he had turned it off when he came into the prison. In fact, he knew he had turned it off because the guard asked if he wanted to leave it at the desk or turn it off. ManMan had opted to simply turn it off, so when it rang as he sat and listened to Jerome's end of the conversation with his mother, he was genuinely shocked.

"Hello?"

"Hello, Rayford, this is Marie." She expected silence and that's what she got. The Man of God didn't know what to say. A full minute passed before he finally responded.

"How are you?"

"I'm fine. I just hadn't heard from you since you left your Mom's and wanted to call."

"Yeah, I should have called before now. I'm sorry. No excuses, no real reason, all I can say is I'm sorry."

"I accept your apology, although I think I understand why you left like you did. It was a lot to take. I hadn't seen you in forever and when I do, I unload all of this weight on you. Jerome. Kal'eal. It was too much, Rayford. I can't blame you for leaving."

"That's good of you to say, Marie, and I Love You for it. But I made a promise to you. I told you whatever I could do to help you find your son, I would do it. Running away wasn't a part of it . . ." She really didn't hear anything much after that. Marie's mind was stuck on those three words, "I Love You." It might have been the urgency of the moment, but it sounded so good to hear The Man of God say that he did love her. The laughter that was rising up in her spirit fought to get out, but she held it in and tried to remain focused on the conversation.

" . . . so I do owe you an apology. Please forgive me, Marie, this time. I'll never run away again. I vow that to you. I'll never run again."

"I believe you, Rayford. And I Love You for you willingness to stand with me, especially now. I should have called you before I left home and told you what I was planning to do. I just started moving and before I knew it, I was on the plane. The lay over in Atlanta was enough time to call you, but I didn't. Didn't know how to tell you . . ."

"Marie, I think I already know what you're trying to tell me. You're on your way to the prison to see Jerome."

"Yes, did he call you again?"

"He didn't have to, I'm here already."

"Here where?"

"At the prison. I'm here talking with Jerome."

His mother had been stern with him before, but Jerome had never heard this tone in her voice. It told him not to argue with her or try to change her mind. So he didn't.

"Okay, Mama, it's alright. Go ahead and bring Kal'eal up here. I don't know how it will all turn out but go ahead and bring him. Marie is already on her way and maybe it's just time for it all to come out in the open – before it's too late and ya'll be left to straighten it out without me. Yeah, go ahead and bring him up here." He kept saying it to convince himself it would be alright. He could get through it. All would be well.

"Well, we'll be up there tomorrow. Soon as your sister get off work and get the children, me and him will get on the train and be up there in about three hours I guess. I tried to get Lois to bring me, but she got to work tomorrow though. But however we have to come, me and Kal'eal will be there tomorrow if the Lord say the same. Do you want me to bring anything else special? I got some flour and stuff in there to make a cake if you feel like you can eat some. You want me to bring you some more fried chicken?"

Jerome knew she was trying to let him know she still loved him and, in her own way, was trying to apologize for speaking so sharply to him. So even though he knew he probably wouldn't be able to keep anything on his stomach, he told her, "Yeah, Mama, that sounds good. I ain't had no good chicken since the last time you brought some. And maybe the cake will be good. Maybe when Marie and Kal'eal get here, we'll have something to celebrate. I'll see you tomorrow, Mama. I Love You."

"I Love You, too, Baby."

"And Mama, thank you."

"You welcome, Baby. You welcome. I'll see you tomorrow."

He hung up the phone and noticed that ManMan was in deep conversation with someone. From the sound of it, someone close to him. He didn't want to eavesdrop, so he tried to get up and make his way back down the ward to give Milfred the phone. The Man of God waived him back into bed and held out his hand for the phone. When Jerome gave it to him, he said into his cell phone, "I'm here with him now." Jerome waited for ManMan to say a name and when he didn't hear one, he mouthed, "Who is it?" He could clearly read the response: "Marie." The Man of God walked down the ward and toward Milfred's desk to return the phone.

"When will you be here? What time I mean?"

"I left the airport about an hour and a half ago. I'll probably stop to get something to eat before too long. That should put me really close before it gets too late. What's the latest I can come in the prison?"

"About 4:00. That's only about a half hour from now."

"I hadn't really planned to go today anyway. I

just wanted to be closer than the airport tomorrow. What time are you leaving?"

"In a little while. Where are you staying tonight?"

"I made a reservation at The Ambassador. It's only fifteen minutes from the prison by the interstate. Where are you staying?"

"I hadn't really planned that far in advance. To tell you the truth, I didn't even know I would be here until I got here."

"Can we share a room at the hotel and still stay saved?" Marie ventured into an area that had plagued her since high school. There had never been any real intimacy between them, but they both knew their desire for each other was strong.

"Well, I don't know if we should even take that chance, but if you can reserve me a room when you get to the hotel, I'd appreciate it. Maybe we can be in the same hotel and be safe. What do you think?"

CHAPTER 25

JEROME HAD DEFINITELY HAD SOME long nights since he'd been in prison, but after ManMan left, the morning seemed further away as the hours passed. Being disturbed to take his late dose of meds was a relief to him. It took his mind off of the day facing him on tomorrow. He didn't know what to do, all of the voices in his head were telling him that the worst would happen: Marie would still be angry, as she should be; Kal'eal would hate him for having withheld the truth for all his life; his mother would get upset and try to make peace – he only hoped her blood pressure wouldn't go up so high like it did at her oldest son's funeral. He was even unsure about how the Man of God would play into everything. Would he remember their conversation about love and forgiveness or would he take sides with Marie and remember the hatred he had before arriving at the prison?

His bed was comfortable, but he couldn't

sleep. The light from the digital clock seemed to be keeping him awake, so he put a towel over it. Still, no sleep would come. He looked at the phone beside the bed with all its numbers and directions, and thought about calling Marie. She was right across the hall. Her parting words had been, "Call me if you need to talk or if you can't sleep. I know I probably won't." And she was right. The walls in her hotel room reflected the bright lights of the television, which was really watching her instead of vice versa. Marie was looking at the movie, but by no means was she watching it. She, like Jerome and ManMan, was playing over and over again in her mind what might happen tomorrow. But regardless of how much they rehearsed, neither she nor ManMan could imagine what God was really doing. Because as of yet, neither of them knew Kal'eal would be there, too.

You know I ain't done this since I was a child, so I just hope You'll hear me. I need Your help. My life ain't worth much and I ain't really asking for nothing for me. This what I got, this AIDS, I deserve it. It's what I brought on myself. That ain't what I need to talk to You about. It's my son and his mama. You already know the situation, so I ain't got to go into all of that with You. But I just want everything to be alright between them. He don't know her, but she know him. And I know she love him. Always has. I was wrong for keeping him from her all these years, just for the hell of it. Excuse me for that. I mean just because I could, I kept a mother and child apart. Just because I'm a mean son of a . . . Anyway, I need You to do whatever You need to so this will go right tomorrow. Let my Mama make it up here alright and let her bring my son. I know I don't have no right to ask You this, but please let him still love me. Don't let my child hate me, God. Don't let my child hate me . . .

. . . I don't hate him, God, but there's still something there. Move it before I see him tomorrow. He's dying and ain't nothing I can do to make him suffer more than he already is. So just move on my heart and take the anger away. When I see him, Father, I don't even want to remember all that stuff he did to me. It's all over with now. It's all passed. He don't owe me nothing. Forgive him, Jesus, for what he did. Give him peace about it. Let him know that You're ready to forgive him and accept him as Your child. Bless him, Father. Help me let him know that I don't hate him no more. Thank You, God, for delivering me from my own hatred. Thank You, Holy Spirit. Speak to Jerome's heart. I just need to know where my child is. That's all I need to know. I need to know where my child is . . .

. . . From his birth, God, You've kept Kal'eal. And even though Marie doesn't know where he is, I know You know. You've known all the time. I don't know why You haven't given her child back to her, but I just trust You, Lord. I believe that You have a purpose and a reason for *everything. When she sees Jerome tomorrow, God, give her a peace that passes all understanding. Let her forget all the pain and release all the anger. Move by Your Spirit and bring peace in the midst of a confused situation. Heal every hurt. Erase every pain. From Marie, from Jerome, even from Kal'eal, wherever he might be. Let the passage be easy for healing. I know You have all Power and I know You can. Move by Your Spirit . . .*

. . . I remember Mama telling me about the Holy Ghost or the Spirit, how it can help you get through things you can't get through on your own. I think that's what I need right now. I need some help. This is too hard for me to do by myself. How I'm go' look Marie in the face after how I treated her? How I'm go' look at my son and still be a man in his eyes, all sick and broke down? He go' remember how I used to hit Marie. He go' hate me, too. I know he is. I need You help, God. I'm scared. I'm for real this time. I need Your help. Help me, please . . .

. . . Please touch his heart and let him not fight. I don't want to spend a minute, not a second, fighting no more. We did enough of that all those years ago. No more fighting, Lord, no more confusion. Whatever You have to do, God, by any means necessary, make us all understand that if You can forgive us, we can surely forgive one another. Bless that Man of God across the hall for being here. Bless him for his obedience to what You commissioned him to do. Bless him because he could have said no and walked away for good, but he didn't.

Bless him because he was willing to stand in the gap for me and talk to Jerome, and try to help me find my child. Just bless him, God. Every way You can find to, bless him. Anything that he's lost, restore it to him. Bless him, Father . . .

. . . What we need is Your blessing and Your Presence. We can't do this by ourselves. There's not enough human ability in either of us to get through this. I know You know that, but I want You to know I know it, too. Out hearts are not strong enough. Our minds are too shallow. Our egos are too big. Our hurts are too deep. Our tongues are too heavy. Our eyes are too full of our own desires. We need You, God. We need You. Show up in that prison like You never have before and be the Power that holds us together and keeps peace. Meet us there, Lord. Go right now and touch Jerome and give him peace. Let him know it's already done. It's already worked out. Give him peace and rest, Holy Spirit. Amen.

He didn't know when, but somewhere in the night, Jerome had fallen into a peaceful sleep. For the first time in many years, two things had happened: he had prayed and he had truly rested. He woke up feeling calm and strangely assured that things would work out alright. The attendant who brought his breakfast and morning meds noticed that something was different about him, but couldn't quite tell what it was. Jerome was smiling and the attendant thought he heard him humming a broken tune. His appetite was good, and he almost finished all of his breakfast.

"What has gotten into you, Mr. Jerome Grayson? I haven't seen you eat or smile like that before. Are you that glad to see me this morning?"

"I wouldn't say all of that now, but I'm just glad to be alive. I don't really know what it is, just that somehow things look better this morning than they did last night. Can't explain it, but I feel good this morning. Real good . . ."

His words trailed off and took the attendant by surprise. He struggled to answer, and finally said, "Alright, stop that now. You be done made me start crying in here or shouting or something. You know it don't take much for me. Just stop that now. The Man of God must have prayed for you when he was here yesterday. You seem like you got a whole new lease on life."

"He didn't pray for me, he just talked to me. I mean really talked to me. In spite of all the reasons he could have had to hate me and be absolutely right, he still came to talk to me. That made me feel good, and I thank God for that . . . ." Before he knew it, he had said out loud what he was feeling in his spirit. He was simply glad that God had begun to do something to help him fix the terrible mess he had made of his life. Somewhere in the night, something had been changed in him. What it was, he honestly couldn't articulate, but he knew, beyond the shadow of a doubt that something had changed.

Marie had been up for hours, praying and crying, crying and praying, and must have changed clothes at least six times already. She wasn't necessarily worried about how she would look. Changing clothes was just something to do. The phone was drawing her attention and beckoned for her to call ManMan. Was it too early? She hoped not as she picked up the phone and dialed the four digits that were both his room number and extension.

"Good morning. Are you up yet?"

"Yes, I've been up for at least three hours, and I don't think I slept but two. How are you this morning?"

"I'm about to jump out of my skin. I've changed clothes more times than any normal person would and it's not even seven o'clock yet. I don't know what I'm going to do until ten o'clock."

"What time does the breakfast buffet begin? Was it six or seven? We can go sit down and have some breakfast, talk, and just relax. Is that good?"

"Yes, I think that'll help. The breakfast started at six thirty. Are you ready now or do you need some time?"

"I'm ready. Just give me about ten minutes. I'm

going to call Daddy and see how he's doing. I need to let them know where I am, too."

"Okay, take your time. Just knock on the door or call when you get ready to go. It's no rush. Take your time."

"Alright, I'll talk to you in a few minutes."

It was very early, but ManMan had a feeling that his father would be up already. He needed to talk with him before his visit with Jerome. The Man of God was unsure of what would happen, how the visit would begin or end, but he knew that he needed to call his daddy. In his mind flashed a memory of when he was in grade school and someone, he couldn't remember who, had bullied him and torn his shirt. He went home and refused to change clothes until his daddy saw what that bully had done to him. ManMan's young ego was sure that Daddy would take off work the next day, go down to the school, and look that bully in the eye and say, "Hey, don't mess with my son no more!"

Contrary to his beliefs, Daddy didn't react at all when he saw the shirt. All through dinner, after he finished his second piece of pie and cup of coffee, he didn't say a word. ManMan ate slowly and stayed at the table as long as his father did. He walked real slow and close to him when he took his plate to the kitchen. Finally, after feeling invisible, ManMan heard the words he was listening for all evening, "What happened to your shirt, Boy?"

"Jimmy David was messing with me and pulled on it and tore it." He used his most pitiful and sad voice.

"And?" his father surprised him with one word that sounded like a question.

"And I told the teacher and she told him to leave me alone."

"You told the teacher, huh?"

"Yes, Sir."

"And what did you think the teacher was supposed to do? Beat him up for you? Take your side in it? Make him leave you alone?"

ManMan, even at the tender age of eight, knew when Daddy started asking questions like that, it wasn't because he really wanted you to answer. And if you did, he would always tell you that you were wrong and then tell you what you should have said. So he didn't answer, but stood there looking at the floor.

Just as he expected, the elder Johnson continued speaking. "I tell you what, the next time you come in here with your shirt tore up and sounding like some pitiful little puppy, you go' have to fight me, too. I ain't saying just get into no fight for nothing, but I am saying you got to learn how to defend yourself and stand up for yourself. You understand what I'm saying to you, Boy?"

"Yes, Sir."

"You keep walking around that school letting this Jimmy David or whoever else push you around, pretty soon everybody go' be pushin' you around. Don't you think so?"

This time ManMan ventured to answer. There was only one question. "Yes, Sir."

"I ain't go' always be here to take up for you, and you don't need to always look to me to do it. When it's something you can't handle, then I'll try my best to help you. Then sometimes I might not. Just depends on what the situation is. This here, this boy at the school, I think that's one you got to handle yourself. If he bigger than you, you better find some friends and all ya'll put him in his place. If you can't find no friends, pick up something . . . . But whatever you do, stand up for yourself. I can't fight your battles for you. You go' be a man one day and right now is the time for you to understand that it ain't go' always be easy. You hear me talking to you, Son?"

"Yes, Sir."

"Do you understand what I'm saying to you?"

"Yes, Sir."

"Alright then. Go on upstairs and get out of them clothes. Take your bath and get ready for bed. I'll be up to tell you about David and Goliath before you go to sleep. Is that alright?" Daddy knew this was ManMan's favorite Bible story and would always brighten up the bleakest situations. With a sly, hesitant smile, the son answered, "Yes, Sir" once again and disappeared down the hall.

"Hey there, now. Your Mama told me it was you, but I didn't know whether to believe her or not. It's been a minute, ain't it?"

"Yes, Sir, it has. I'm sorry about that. I should have called way before now."

"Don't worry about it, Son. I told your Mama you'd call when you could. Sooner or later, I knew you'd call. How you gettin' along? You in Atlanta?"

"No, Sir, I'm actually in Illinois. I came here to go to the prison where Jerome Grayson is, Marie's husband." He wanted to say more but decided to wait for his father's reaction to the first bit of news.

"Is that right? Your Mama told me that Marie was headed up that way herself to see him. To talk to him about her baby. Did ya'll go up there together?"

"No, Sir. I didn't even know she was coming and she didn't know I would already be here. I was actually sitting talking to Jerome when he got the message that she was coming."

"You don't say? How did it go with him? Did you find out where the child is?"

"No, Sir, we didn't really get that far yesterday. After he found out Marie was coming, it was time for me to leave. She called me on my cell phone while I was in the prison and told me she was here. I told her I was here, too, and we stayed at the hotel last night. We're going back to see Jerome today. I'm hoping he'll tell her where Ka'leal is today. That's what she really wants to know."

"I hope so too. It must be a terrible thing to have a child in the world and not know where he is. It must be a terrible thing. I pray God he'll tell her what she need to know. And you don't forget what I told you. God put you back in Marie's life for a reason – to stand by her and to help her. Do all you can to help her find her child. Don't leave her to go through this by herself."

"No, Sir, I won't leave her again. When I left home, I did it wrong. God really dealt with me about that. I mean I couldn't sleep, couldn't find no kind of peace. Couldn't concentrate on work. I was miserable."

"Son, that's what you always go' be anytime you step outside of God's Will. His Will is perfect and He knows what He's doing. You can't second guess Him. Can't afford to. It'll backfire on you every time."

"You're right about that, Daddy. You are

absolutely right. . . . How are you doing? That's what I called to find out. How you feeling?"

"Oh, I'm doing just fine. Much better now that I know you alright. I went to the store to get my medicine. Talked to Dr. Barrette again. He still want me to go through with the chemotherapy, but he don't bother me about it as much now. I think he finally believe what I'm saying. So far, though, I'm feeling real good. No complaints at all."

"Would you tell me if there were?"

"Probably not." They both laughed, each realizing once again how well they knew each other, how much they loved each other, and how much they needed each other.

"How's Mr. Johnson doing? Did you get a chance to talk to him?"

"He says he's doing fine. I'll have to take his word for it. He sounded good. He said to tell you that everything would be alright. He just 'got a feeling,' he said. You know how he is when he starts talking like that. I heard the tears in his voice when he said it. And usually when he starts crying, with one tear rolling down the side of his face, whatever he says comes to pass. So I have to believe he might know something we don't."

"That's good enough for me. Between your Daddy crying, me praying all night, and God hearing, I've got a feeling, too."

"I thought I heard somebody speaking in tongues last nigh. Was that you?"

"Oh Lord, are you serious? Was I that loud? Could you hear me for real?"

Before he could answer, his laugh gave him away. "Naw, I'm just messin' with you. I didn't hear you. I wouldn't have been able to hear your prayers for the sound of my own anyway. Every time I tried to go to sleep, I would think of something else to say or to just pour out of my spirit to God. Finally, about three hours ago, I went to sleep."

"I know what you mean. We must have been on the same prayer schedule. But you know what? I think it helped me more than anything else. Don't get me wrong now, I was praying for all of us, you, me, Jerome, Ka'leal, but when I was through, I felt so free. The anger and hatred I had for Jerome seems so far away now. All I want to do now is let him know I forgive him. Is that crazy or what?"

"It's not crazy at all. God is doing something, Marie. I don't know what, but He's definitely moving in all of this. When I went in to see Jerome yesterday, I thought I would be thinking about how to keep from being as nasty as I could to him. I just knew it was going to be hard to sit down and talk to him. But when I saw him, how frail and fragile he looked, I don't know, something inside me just changed. In a minute, before I could even tell it was happening, I couldn't be mad at him no more. My whole spirit, my mind, my heart, everything that had told me to hate him was now telling me I had to love him. It was the most amazing thing I have ever experienced in my life. And I know it was nobody but the Holy Spirit moving, working on me and in me. I'll have to be honest with you, Marie, it felt real good not to hate him. To be free to have compassion on him. To understand, to realize, that he's just a man. Weak. Vulnerable. Afraid. In need of love and forgiveness. Just like me. He's just a man."

CHAPTER 26

HE WONDERED WHO WOULD BE the first to arrive this morning. It probably wouldn't be his mama, since she had to come all the way up to the prison on the bus, she and Ka'leal. They wouldn't get there until after twelve he was sure. The Man of God would probably come first. Had he talked to Marie yet? Maybe they would come together. That, Jerome thought to himself, would surely make things easier. He had felt calm and confident this morning when he woke up, but now, after the painful walk to the shower, the water that stung his sagging flesh and punished his fragile bones, he was sitting in the bed feeling scared again.

Now if You go' help me through this, I need You to stay in it. Last night and this morning I felt good, but now I'm doubting if I should even go through with any of this. Maybe I should just tell Johnson and Milfred I don't want to see nobody, not even my mama and my son. That would take care of it all. They could all sit out there and decide what to do on their own. Just leave me out of it . . .

Jerome's fear had begun to make him imagine how badly it could all go. Marie still hating him. His son looking at the sorry excuse for a man, a father, he had turned out to be. His mother sitting by, crying and praying, or cursing herself for having birthed such a pitiful child. And then The Man of God, who had never done any wrong in his life, standing there in the middle of it all, judging and condemning him for all he had done to Marie and Ka'leal. It was too much for him. He was sick. This wasn't something he had to do. Nobody in the prison would make him do it. He didn't have to receive any visitors if he didn't want to. But then, in the middle of his argument in favor of not seeing Marie, ManMan, Ka'leal, or his mother, he heard the words of a song they used to sing when he was in Mississippi. That was the only time he really went to church because his auntie made him go. *"This too will pass . . . This too will pass . . . ."*

Those are the only words he heard echoing from those childhood memories, but it was enough. The fear would go away. Everything would work out. He would do this. As a last attempt to do something good before his life was over, he would do this. He owed it to everyone on the way to the prison, and he would not die without paying the debt. He couldn't go back and erase all of the stupid, irresponsible, hurtful, downright evil that he had done, but while he was facing his own mortality a little more everyday, he could ask Marie for forgiveness, offer his hand to The Man of God, say thanks to his mother, and tell his son that he loved him. These things, he could – and would – do before he died.

Help me, God. I need You to help me get through this. I'm begging You. Please help me say the right thing and do the right thing. I give up. I ain't go' fight You no more. I've been so wrong in my life, but I still need You. The Man of God, the one You sent here, said that You would love me no matter what. He said that I couldn't be evil enough for You not to love me. He said Your love didn't know no end. I'm depending on that to be true. Somehow, some way, I need You to give me the strength I need to do this right. I'm scared, but I just don't want them to hate me no more. I'm sorry. I'm so sorry for everything I did to them. Just let them forgive me. Just don't let them hate me no more. I don't want to die knowing that. I can't ask You to make them love me, just let them forgive me. That's all. Just let them forgive me. I need this, God. I can't tell You how much. Just let them forgive me. I can die in peace if I know that . . .

To ManMan's surprise and relief, Johnson was on duty. He must have pulled double shifts or something. Whatever it was, The Man of God was glad to see his possible distant cousin when he and Marie pulled into the prison's main parking lot. This time is was not he, but Marie who needed time to sit in the car and get herself together. She hadn't said anything since they got in the car and started on the interstate toward the prison. ManMan didn't want to force conversation, and she didn't offer any. She just looked out the window. Every so often, he could see her out of the corner of his eye wipe her face. She was crying. Everything in him wanted to ask if she was okay, but he knew she wasn't. This was the first time she would see the man who had beaten her, almost killed her more than once, and who had caused her child to be taken away from her. How could she be okay?

When they did pull into the parking lot, ManMan just sat there with the car running. He knew that turning it off might have been a sign that he was ready to go in. And he was, but was Marie? After about five minutes of silence, she took a deep breath and wiped her face one last time.

"Well, we're here. Might as well go on in and . . . ."

"Are you sure you're ready? We can sit here as long as we need to."

"That guard over there might not agree with you on that."

"Oh, he'll be okay. He probably remembers me

from yesterday. When I pulled in, I sat out here for what must have been a good fifteen minutes. Then he had to come and ask me what I was doing. He'll remember, so take your time. We'll go in when and not until you are ready to go in, okay?"

"Okay, I'm ready." With that Marie opened her door before ManMan could get out and come around to do it for her. She moved quickly, scared that all her courage would leave her if she stopped or slowed down any. They got to the gate and Johnson greeted The Man of God with familiarity.

"Hey there, Cousin. I see you back again, and you brought somebody with you. This must be your wife." Immediately sensing a bit of uneasiness, Johnson corrected himself, "Now look at me. Don't know you from Eve's cousin Sue and already done paired you up with this other Johnson here. I'm sorry about that, Ma'am."

His sincerity and warmth comforted Marie, and she smiled at his embarrassment. "That's alright, Sir. I don't mind. But no, I'm not his wife. Just a friend . . . ."

"Yes, Ma'am. If you just sign this sheet here, right under The Man of God, you both can go through this gate to the second one and they'll let ya'll on in." He looked at the sign-in sheet and saw Marie's last name. His tone of voice after he saw it was at once questioning and pitying. "Mrs. Grayson? You're not Mrs. *Jerome* Grayson, are you?"

"Actually, I am, and that's who I've, we've come to see. So can we go on to the other gate now?"

"Yes, Ma'am. Go right ahead." Johnson watched them all the way up to the other gate, then got on the radio and told the guard there to let them straight through. "They here to see Grayson. That's a preacher and Grayson's wife. He must not be doing so good. Let them straight though and call ahead to the others. Tell them I'm vouching for both of them. Just let 'em straight through. Might not be no time to waste."

Indeed, there was no time to waste. Not because Jerome had gotten any worse but because of the urgency of what was about to happen. For the first time in ten years, he and Marie would be face to face, and although she didn't know it, she would see her son again. The blessing and miracle she had been praying for was taking shape and would fully manifest that day. She would see her son. But first, she would see her husband. It felt strange to think about it that way, but while she was being taken through one prison door after another, that's the only way Marie could think of herself. She didn't know whether it was because the first guard had put the phrase in her head or what, but all she could think as she walked was that she was going to see her husband. With the man she loved walking by her side, she was going to see her husband.

The effeminate attendant ManMan remembered from yesterday met them at the entrance to the ward. "Good morning, Preacher Man. Hello Ma'am, how are you?" He didn't give either of them time to respond. "Can you all just sit right here for just a minute? I need to attend to Mr. Grayson before you go in. I think he pushed himself too hard this morning and had a little accident. He was so excited that he ate more than he has in months. His stomach couldn't handle it, though. So if you all will give me a good ten minutes, he'll be ready to receive you." He turned to walk away, but then stopped dead in his tracks, as if he had hit a brick wall. He snapped back around and looked right at Marie, "You've got to be the one he's been thinking about and talking about every since I've been seeing about him. You've got to be Marie. Yeah, that's you. Just like he said, you are beautiful and your soul is good. I just met you, but I can feel that you have a good soul. He'll be glad to see you. Yep, you must be the one."

Again, he did not give Marie the chance to respond, not that she could have anyway. She was in shock. Jerome had mentioned her to someone else? Had said she was beautiful and had a good soul? From the way he had treated her when they were together, she didn't think he thought that much of her, much less that she was beautiful and good. But he had. That's what had drawn him to her in the beginning. She was sweet, pure, naturally beautiful. Didn't need all the make-up girls their age were trying to wear when they were just in high school. They looked more like street-walkers than young ladies. Marie stood out among them. She was always trying to help somebody, take the underdog's side, make it better for the kids everybody else picked on. She was a breath of fresh air to Jerome when he went to Mississippi that summer. And he hoped she could find some way to forgive him for treating her like she wasn't.

Sweet, the attendant, guessed that Jerome had eaten too much. Jerome knew better. He had barely eaten a bowl of oatmeal and a dry piece of toast for breakfast. It wasn't the food that made him sick. It was nothing but nerves. The mutant butterflies were in his stomach reeking havoc. Every time he thought he was okay, they started flying around stirring things up again. Sweet had to help him change clothes two times already. This was the third and hopefully the last. He wondered if anyone had made it yet. No one had been on the ward to say so, and surely Sweet would have let him know.

"Alright now, Mr. Jerome Cantrell Grayson, you better quit all this. You got people out there waiting for you. You don't want them to see you like this, do you? Now let's get this soiled gown off of you. I want this to be the last time I have to come in and help you change now. Do we have an understanding?" Sweet was being himself and trying to make things urgent and light at the same time.

"Did you say somebody was out there already? Who is it? Is it a man or a woman? It's not my mama is it?" Despite the physical pain he was in, Jerome moved swiftly to get into the clean gown and the house coat Sweet had swiped from somewhere. "Hey, where'd you get this robe? This ain't regular prison issue I know."

"Don't you worry about where it came from. You just put it on. We can't have you looking like a bum with The Preacher Man here again today, now can we?"

"Oh, so it's Rayford that's back . . ."

"Yes, but he's not by himself. There's a beautiful woman out there. It can't be nobody but Marie. She looks just like you said she did. But she's even more beautiful. It can't be nobody but her. That's why I went in my private stash and got this robe for you. You ready to see them? You feel alright?"

"Yeah, I'm ready. Wait, give me that comb out the drawer. How does my hair look? Is any mouthwash or anything in there? What about one of those little cloth things you use when I can't brush my teeth? Any of them in there? You got a wet washcloth so I can wash my face again?"

"If you don't calm down, you go be right back where you started from, and I ain't got another robe for you to put on." Sweet's mouth was saying one thing, but faster than Jerome could ask for things, he had them for him. "Wait a minute. Let me see that comb. Head looking like a bowl of popcorn. You should have told me you had people coming. We could have gotten you a hair cut before today. See how you do? You don't tell me nothing . . ."

"I didn't know they were all coming today. My mama and my son coming this afternoon, too."

"Oh Jesus, she go' swear we ain't taking care of you . . ." As he resigned from trying to do anything more to Jerome's miniature afro, Sweet heaved a deep sigh. "Alright, that's all I can do. It look alright though. But you should have told me. Are you ready now? I told them ten minutes and here you done took at least thirty. You ready?"

"Yeah, I'm ready. You can bring them in." Sweet turned to leave but again stopped for the brick wall.

"Grayson, just be real. As hard as it might be, just be real and be honest. That's the only thing that will help settle all of this. Say what you've got to say and don't put up that old fake front. Don't look at me like that. I know you. I know how you can try to be hard. Don't do that this time. This is your chance, the one you said you wanted. Do you remember that? Well here it is. Don't mess it up, okay?"

"Okay, Man, I hear you. And Sweet, thank you."

"You know it, Brother." He disappeared outside the ward door, leaving it open behind him and Jerome looking nervously for his visitors to enter.

"Hello Jerome, how are you?"

"I'm feeling okay. How are you?"

"I am well today."

To his surprise and hers, Marie had come onto the ward alone. She told The Man of God she needed to do this by herself. Jerome was still her husband and she was still his wife. If she had made the choice to marry him and leave Mississippi with him, surely she could sit beside him in a hospital bed by herself. She wasn't afraid anymore and the anger had gone to a place where she couldn't find it anymore. Remember it, yes. But feel it, not any more.

Yes, she was more beautiful than he had remembered, and certainly than he could ever describe. Jerome remembered all over again why he had loved her.

"The nurse said that Rayford was with you. Did he decide not to come in?"

"No, I asked him to wait outside. I thought we needed to talk about some things alone first. Don't you agree?"

"Yeah, you're right."

After a moment of awkwardness, Jerome began. "Marie, the first thing I want to do is say I'm sorry. I know I've said it so many times before, when we were in Chicago, but this time, I'm for real. When Rayford came to see me yesterday, it made me realize some things. Even when I talked to him on the phone and said all of that stupid stuff about the lawyer, I knew then something had to give. Everything in me has been turning upside down since then. It's like I had to finally say to myself how wrong I was and how much I needed to see you and say I'm sorry for everything. For getting you pregnant, for taking you away from Mississippi, for keeping you from it, from home and people who loved you. I'm sorry for all of that, Marie." His emotions began to overwhelm him, so Jerome stopped talking. He hoped and prayed Marie would understand and believe he was being as real and honest as he could. His words were tangled and confused, but he hoped she could hear and see his sincerity.

"Jerome, I do believe you. You don't have to try to convince me. Let me just say before I decided to come to Chicago, when Rayford was on the phone with you, I was so angry at you. When I heard you mention the lawyer and everything, my hatred for you and all the memories of what you did to me came back with a vengeance. I swore I would never forgive you, could never forgive you, much less sit down and have a conversation with you. The only thing you could tell me was where Kal'eal is, and other than that, you could die and go straight to hell for all I cared." The mention of Kal'eal made Marie's eyes water and her throat tight. But she kept going.

"But then, I don't know what, but something happened. Maybe it was the dream I had. You and I were in front of our child asking for forgiveness. Yes, both of us. I should have left the first time you hit me, but I was too proud and didn't want anybody to know I had made a mistake in marrying you. You should have never laid your hands on me in anger, either. So both of us were to blame for losing Kal'eal. And in the dream, we were both in front of him asking for forgiveness."

As she spoke, images of how baldy he had treated Marie flashed through Jerome's mind. The time he had brought Josie to the apartment for her to sleep with him. The time he beat her for not having food ready when he got home. When he told her she was going to prostitute herself or else. The many, many times he had just beaten her for no reason at all. His soul ached at the suffering he had inflicted on her. Worst of all, he had caused her to lose Kal'eal and had, for the 9 years since, kept him away from her. Of all the things he had done, that, he was sure, was the one for which she would never forgive him once she found out.

His eyes were so bright, and he still had that crooked little smile she remembered. Before he came into the ward or even got close to her, Marie knew it was Kal'eal. Her spirit leapt inside her, and her heart felt like it would jump right out of her chest. She didn't breathe until he was standing right in front of her and then she took only shallow, labored breaths, like she was giving birth to him all over again.

His grandmother, whom he called Mudda, had talked with him the day before and while they were on the train this morning. First she told him that he was going to see his daddy. But then she started crying like she did in church, and Kal'eal knew there was something else, too.

"Mudda, why you crying? You know I ain't scared to go to see my daddy. That prison don't scare me." At eleven and a half, he had gotten the art of comforting his grandmother down to a science. When she seemed worried about a bill, he would say, "You can take the money for my shoes and pay it, Mudda. I can wear these for a long time.

They ain't too little or nothing," even though they were cramping his toes. When she coughed one time too many or rubbed her hands with Ben Gay, he would say, "Mudda, I told you to take it easy. I'm going to help Mrs. Jenkins down at the store. You don't have to go clean up no houses today." Kal'eal loved his grandmother and would do anything he could to help her. To him, she was his mother. The only one he had ever really known.

So when she mentioned going to see his daddy, he didn't think anything of it. But when she said calmly, "And your Mama's go' be there, too," his eleven and a half, almost twelve-year-old mind reeled. He vaguely remembered a woman's face, looking over another woman's shoulder and telling the face he remembered to come go with him. Whenever he would ask Mudda about it, she would just shoo him away or say he must have dreamed it. But now, he was standing in front of the face he remembered and sometimes dreamed about. She didn't say anything, but was breathing hard like Mudda did right before she shouted in church. Was this his real mama?

"Hello Kal'eal. How are you?"

"Fine." He still didn't know who she was for sure but the memory of her face became clearer and stronger the longer he looked at her.

"Do you know who I am? Do you remember me, Kal'eal?"

"Yes, Ma'am. You my mama."

Before she knew it, Marie was on her knees in front of her son, embracing him. At first, he did not return her embrace. She prayed to herself, *God please let him love me.* As the words went from her heart to God's ear, Kal'eal put his arms around her neck and said, "It's alright, Mama, you don't have to cry no more. We're back together again." As she looked in his eyes, trying to find words, Marie's beautiful child comforted his mother, just as her mother had comforted her when she found her way home so many years ago. He wiped the tears from her face with his shirt tail and said, "Don't cry Mama. I'm alright. Mudda took care of me, but now, you can be my Mama again. Is that alright, Mama?"

The Story Continues with Book II . . .
"In God's House: A Story about Redemption"

Printed in the United States
By Bookmasters